"How old asked E...

"She's eight months."

"Gah!"

Rosie shrieked at the top of her voice and flung her rattle straight at Morgan. He held it out to her again. Two pairs of sapphire eyes locked for endless seconds, the baby's holding a mixture of curiosity and suspicion, Morgan's impossible to read, before a plump hand reached out and snatched the rattle back.

"And gah to you, too," Morgan returned with a flicker of amusement.

Ellie turned away to hide the hot, betraying tears that stung her eyes. Morgan's tiny smile had shattered her composure.

Would that smile still be there if he knew the truth?

"She's a pretty little thing," Morgan said. "I assume that she takes after her father?"

Passion™

in

Harlequin Presents®

Looking for sophisticated stories that **sizzle**?
Wanting a read that has a little extra **spice**?

Pick up a Presents _Passion_™ novel—
where **seduction** is _guaranteed!_

Coming in March:

the start of a thrilling new duet by **Miranda Lee!**
A Secret Vengeance
Harlequin Presents #2236

Kate Walker

HIS MIRACLE BABY

Passion™

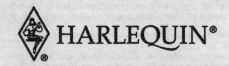

TORONTO • NEW YORK • LONDON
AMSTERDAM • PARIS • SYDNEY • HAMBURG
STOCKHOLM • ATHENS • TOKYO • MILAN • MADRID
PRAGUE • WARSAW • BUDAPEST • AUCKLAND

ISBN 0-373-12232-2

HIS MIRACLE BABY

First North American Publication 2002.

Copyright © 2001 by Kate Walker.

This edition published by arrangement with Harlequin Books S.A.

® and TM are trademarks of the publisher. Trademarks indicated with ® are registered in the United States Patent and Trademark Office, the Canadian Trade Marks Office and in other countries.

Visit us at www.eHarlequin.com

Printed in U.S.A.

CHAPTER ONE

It was the moment Ellie had been dreading most. The worst moment in a day she had been anticipating with a sense of something close to horror for almost a month now.

No, that wasn't strictly true. The actual fact was that she had feared this moment for around a year and a half. Ever since she had left Morgan and fled here to Cornwall, she had had the worry at the back of her mind that one day he might come back into her life.

And that day was now. The thought was enough to still her footsteps, bring her to a stumbling halt, a thousand frantic butterflies fluttering wildly inside her stomach as she stared at the short stretch of path that led away from her, towards the cottage.

'I can't! I can't do it.'

Morgan was just around that corner. And he was waiting for her to appear. Though of course he didn't actually know it was *Ellie* he was waiting for. And the thought of his probable reaction lifted all the tiny hairs on her skin in a shivering reaction to the panic that clenched all her nerves tight.

'Come on, Eleanor,' she reproached herself. 'What can he do to you?'

He didn't have to *do* anything, that was the trouble. Morgan could mess up her life, her mind, her *heart*, simply by existing, and, no matter how she tried, nothing would change that.

No!

Pushing a hand through the golden blonde length of her hair, she squared her slim shoulders resolutely.

'Get a move on...'

Once more she addressed herself out loud. It was the only way to drown out the endless chattering of the inner voice of fear and unhappiness.

'Just go!'

Somehow the command gave her the impetus to move, one step following the other, her determination growing, adding force, speed to her movements until at last she swung round the corner in a rush.

The sleek, powerful Alfa Romeo parked incongruously on the unmade road outside the small cottage told its own story. If she had been in any possible doubt, had harboured any weak, faint hope that the Morgan Stafford who had arranged for a six-month rental could possibly be someone other than the man she dreaded seeing, then that, and the sight of the tall, dark figure standing beside it, immediately disabused her.

She had forgotten just how big he was. Big and powerful, with a whipcord strength that made her mouth dry just to think of it. In well-worn jeans, tight as a second skin, and an equally elderly, faded, soft denim shirt that clung lovingly to the strong lines of his shoulders and arms, he wouldn't have been taken by anyone for the latest star in the literary firmament and a strong contender for an Oscar for the screenplay of his award-winning thriller.

He was leaning against the rough stone wall of the cottage, long legs crossed at the ankles, arms folded across his powerful chest in a gesture of controlled impatience. But as she approached, more slowly now, he straightened up, somehow managing to convey a sense of disapproval with every movement as he glanced pointedly at his watch.

'You're late!' were the first words she had heard from him in what seemed like a lifetime.

Morgan saw Ellie coming down the path towards him and

felt his insides clench in instant response to just the sight of her.

She hadn't changed. The afternoon sun glinted on the golden length of her hair, warming the peach softness of her skin to an enticing glow. Her tall, shapely body was enhanced by the neat red skirt that clung to the curve of her hips, the crisp white shirt, open at the neck to give a provocative glimpse of the slender neck that had always delighted him in the past.

She was still the most beautiful woman he had ever seen. The woman who had haunted his dreams by night, tormenting him with a thousand potently erotic images, so that he woke with his heart and head pounding, his body slick with sweat, and the ache of need clawing at him like a pain.

He had to say something. But what did you say to the woman who had, metaphorically at least, kicked you in the guts before walking out of the life you shared without a backward glance?

The life he had thought they'd shared.

The small correction altered his mood at once. The nostalgic feeling vanished as anger rushed over it, dark and thick and hot.

'You're late!'

That brought her head up sharp as he had known it would. The neat chin lifted determinedly, stunning amber eyes flashing gold behind their lush shield of long, thick lashes—impossibly dark for someone with her colouring. This was the way she'd looked the first moment he'd seen her. She'd knocked him for six then and if he didn't get a grip on himself she'd do it again.

'I'm late? I think not! If anything, *you* are early. We said three o'clock and it's…it's…'

Words failed Ellie as she stared at her watch in stunned confusion. Of all the times for the battery to die, it had to go and do it now!

'It's very nearly half past,' Morgan supplied for her as she glared at the offending watch, shaking her wrist roughly in a vain attempt to get it started again. 'I see your time-keeping hasn't got any better over the past eighteen months.'

He had come closer as he'd spoken, moving between her and the sun so that his long body cast a shadow over her as she concentrated fiercely on the unmoving second hand on her watch.

Don't look at him! *Don't look!* she told herself fiercely. Don't even risk it until you're more under control!

Every inch of skin on her body felt as if it were afflicted by prickling pins and needles, and with the once dearly familiar scent of his body tantalising her nostrils she had to struggle to hide her instinctive response. Electricity sizzled along her nerves, making her heart beat a crazy, uneven tattoo. If she looked into his face she would be lost for ever.

And so in spite of her hunger, the aching need to see just once more the features of the man who had taken total possession of her heart and never let it go, she kept her gaze stubbornly averted, watching him only out of the corners of her eyes.

'But if you will insist on wearing that decrepit old thing, then I suppose you can't expect it to be accurate.'

'I happen to *like* this watch!' Ellie retorted defensively. It was also the only one she could afford, but she wasn't going to admit that to him. 'And living and working on a farm, I wouldn't have much use for anything more expensive.'

'True,' Morgan conceded. 'Though I have to admit that a farm in rural Cornwall was really the last place I ever expected to find you.'

'I...'

Her resolution failed her as surprise forced her gaze upwards, to focus on the hard-boned face, all her fears realised as she felt the thudding shock to her system.

Dear heaven, but he looked good! So stunningly, devastatingly good.

After all those months of abstinence, the hunger that swamped her was like a raging tide, sweeping everything before it and threatening to throw her thought processes into total chaos.

'*Expected* to find...? Y-you *knew*!' she forced herself to stammer. 'You were expecting me all the time. So the story that you were here to do research was pure make-believe.'

It made her blood run cold in horror at the idea.

'Not completely,' Morgan returned imperturbably. 'I do have research to do for my next book. And I've tried hotels but I just can't work in them. So renting a place to live in seemed the next best idea.'

'But you could rent anywhere you like—there are many more houses, all much bigger and better than this cottage! You could easily afford any one of them—you could even buy one of them if you wanted to! Why did you have to come here?'

'This place suits me. I don't need space—somewhere to eat, sleep and work is all I want. But to work I need quiet and...'

His narrow-eyed glance took in the wooded surroundings, the rutted path that led to the cottage, the distant view of the sea.

'They really don't come much quieter than this.'

His half smile challenged her to make more of it than that. But there *was* more to make of it, Ellie could have no doubt. Too late, she recognised the clues that her tension had made her miss the first time.

There had been his total lack of surprise at her appearance. His total lack of anything, just that cold, hard, assessing stare that had been fixed on her as she'd walked the last few yards. He had not been expecting just anyone. He had known very well who would come to hand over the key, show him round the cottage. He had been expecting her, and her alone.

And that begged the question—*why?*

'Just what are you doing here, Morgan?'

She had forgotten just how blue his eyes were until now when, up close, she found herself seared by their sapphire blaze, her own angry glare caught and held transfixed, unable to look away.

'Perhaps I came to look up an old friend.'

'Friend!' she scorned the word cynically. 'We were never *friends*. Things moved so fast at the start that we never had time for friendship. And you were certainly not in the least bit *friendly* when you told me to go—to get out of your life and stay out of it for good.'

'I didn't feel friendly,' Morgan growled savagely, a black scowl darkening his face. 'I couldn't wait to see the back of you.'

'A fact which you made perfectly plain.' Remembered pain roughened the edge of her voice.

'Well, what did you expect? After all, you'd just told me that you'd been seeing someone else.'

She hadn't actually told him that. It had been a conclusion he had jumped to, and in order to protect herself she had let him think it. By that point she had been too worn down, too miserable to fight him any more.

'Which brings us back to my question. Precisely why are you here?'

This time his smile was icy, fiendish, tinged with a danger that set her teeth on edge.

'Perhaps I'm planning an old lovers' reunion.'

That smile did terrible things to what little was left of Ellie's composure.

'Well, you can forget that idea straight away!' she flung

at him. 'I'm not interested in a reunion or any such thing. The only thing I am to you is an ex-lover, with the emphasis very definitely on the *ex*, and that's the way I intend it to stay. If I could have done, I would have sent someone else here in my place today, but just because I'm here doesn't mean you can interpret it to your advantage!'

The look he turned on her was dark with contempt, searing over her skin like lightning.

'Might I suggest that you wait until you're invited, my dear Ms Thornton?' he tossed at her in a voice so laden with acid that it seemed to strip a protective layer from her skin, leaving her even more vulnerable than before.

Her certainty that Morgan had some private, hidden agenda was growing by the second. And that being so, she knew that this could never work. She could never cope with him living in the cottage, with waking up every morning knowing that he was here, living in fear of a meeting every single day.

Studiously ignoring his interjection she snatched at a half-formed idea as it presented itself.

'Well, I'm sorry, but I'm afraid there's a slight problem...'

'A problem? What sort of a problem?'

'The—the cottage... It's double booked. Someone else has the tenancy for the next...'

Her voice deserted her as she saw the way his beautiful mouth thinned in anger, his adamant shake of his dark head rejecting her desperate bluff even before she'd managed to express it.

'Then ''someone else'' will have to find somewhere else to stay.'

'But they can't! They...'

'Don't fight me on this, Ellie,' Morgan warned. 'You won't like the consequences if you do. The tenancy is mine—signed and paid for—and with a cheque that was

cleared even before I set off from London. So if you have
any ideas of backing out, I warn you that you will find
things very uncomfortable. Do I make myself clear?'

'Crystal.'

What else could she say? He didn't have to put his threat
into words. She could read it in the cold brilliance of his
eyes, the ruthless determination that set his strong jaw hard
against any hope of appeal.

And she couldn't risk that threat being made real. Money
was desperately tight on the farm, and the idea of setting
up the holiday cottages to bring in some much-needed income was a new one. It had taken a huge investment to
bring the old buildings up to scratch. That was why Henry
had been so delighted when he'd taken Morgan's near end
of season booking.

'No—I'm sure it can be sorted out. We'll find a way
round...'

'*We?*' Morgan demanded sharply. 'I spoke to a Mr
Knightley on the phone.'

'Henry.' Ellie nodded, her expression warming slightly.
'He owns the farm.'

And Henry knew nothing about her own former relationship with Morgan. So of course he had seen no reason at
all to hesitate when Morgan had rung up asking about the
tenancy of Meadow Cottage.

'He's married to Nan—to my grandmother.'

Just for a moment the stiff mask slipped from his face,
revealing a look of genuine astonishment.

'*Marion?*'

It would be a shock, Ellie reflected, a touch of amusement
breaking through the tension that held her slim body taut
and stiff. The last time he had seen her grandmother had
been almost two years ago when she had been the widowed
Mrs Thornton. Even her own family had been stunned by

the whirlwind romance that had ensued from Marion's meeting with Henry Knightley.

'She married again in November last year. Just after...'

Frantically she caught the words up, terrified at what she had been about to reveal.

'Just two months after she met Henry,' she amended awkwardly, painfully conscious of everything she was holding back.

By mentioning Henry Knightley, she had moved the conversation onto very dangerous ground. Morgan might know nothing about Henry, other than the phone conversation he'd had with the older man, but Henry's grandson was a totally different matter. Pete Bedford was the man Morgan believed that she had left him for. The man she had allowed Morgan to think was her new lover in order to cover up the truth.

'So is that how you came to be here? You came with Marion?'

'No, I was here first. I was helping Henry out and Nan came to visit. She met Henry and the rest is history.'

The same could have been said about herself and Morgan, she reflected miserably. Their relationship had followed much of the same heady pattern.

They had met, fallen head over heels for each other, become lovers, and moved in together in exactly the same time span as her grandmother and Henry. But the major difference was that at no point at all had Morgan shown any inclination to want to make any other commitment to her. Marriage, and all that went along with it, had very definitely not been in his plans for the future.

She had been prepared to put up with that. Loving him so desperately, she hadn't asked for more than he'd been willing to give. She had lived with him, shared his life, his bed, and at first that had been enough.

But then things had changed, forcing her into a decision that had torn her heart in two.

'Well, if you're stopping, you'll need these...'

Reaching into her pocket, she pulled out a bunch of keys and waved them, letting the ring that held them dangle from one finger. The faint jingling noise they made added a welcome note of carelessness, one she tried to match as she went on, 'I think you'll find Meadow Cottage very comfortable. I hope you enjoy your stay.'

There, now she'd done her duty—more than her duty! She'd met Morgan as arranged, faced him, spoken to him, and by doing so she'd also confronted her own private demons.

And she'd survived.

If she could just get out now, then she might be able to hold herself together. If she went home...

Home...

A sudden wave of devastating longing swept over her. The need to see Rosie, to hold her daughter's small, warm body close, to inhale the sweet baby scent of her, to hear her soft breathing, was so powerful that it almost overwhelmed her.

It was because of Rosie that she had had to leave Morgan in the first place, something that had come close to destroying her but which had seemed the only way out. Faced with a choice that had been no choice at all, she had been torn between the two people that she loved most in all the world. And she had had to choose Rosie.

Rosie was her world now, all that she had left after losing her relationship with Morgan and the future she had dreamed of. But if Morgan ever found out the truth, then that world was likely to come crashing down round her ears, and she couldn't even begin to imagine what her future would be after that.

CHAPTER TWO

'MR STAFFORD will you please take the keys?'

He'd waited just too long for Ellie's peace of mind. His silence and the way he was watching her, blue eyes slightly narrowed against the sun, made her feel desperately uneasy, the tangled mass of knots in her stomach tightening with every uneven heartbeat.

'The keys...' she repeated with as much emphasis as she dared. 'I have to be going.'

'No.'

It came so softly, almost thrown away, that for a moment or two she wasn't at all sure she had heard him right and frowned her confusion.

'What...?' Bewildered she looked up at him, golden eyes wide in shock and confusion. 'Mr Stafford—I...'

Did she know what it did to him when she looked at him like that? Morgan wondered. Did she know how it twisted deep inside him to see those amazing eyes burn with rejection where once he had seen them burn with love for him— or with what he had believed was love? Did she know how it felt to see her so anxious to leave when in the past it had seemed that she couldn't have enough of him? Couldn't protest her love for him often enough.

Or had all that been a pretence too?

'The name is Morgan,' he declared with cold precision. 'And you go when I say you can—not before.'

That brought a flare of defiance into her flashing gaze.

'But I have to go!'

'No.'

Dammit, it had taken months to get to his moment. Had

15

he spent so long looking for her only to have her turn and run at the very first meeting? She was as edgy as a cat on hot bricks, and it wasn't just as a result of seeing him again. She was hiding something and he was determined to find out what.

'I only want what I'm entitled to.'

'Entitled?'

The need to see Rosie was uppermost in her mind, making it impossible to think straight. She knew that her daughter was safe and well cared for with Marion who doted on her first great-grandchild, but it wasn't for Rosie's sake that she wanted to be with her. It was for her own.

One look at her baby daughter would remind her why she was in the hateful position of lying to the man she had loved.

Morgan's slow smile mocked her tense question, the spark of uncertainty in her eyes.

'The contract said that I would be met, given the keys—and shown round the property.'

'Shown round! Oh, come on! I mean, look at it...'

The gesture of her hand to indicate the cottage beside them was wilder than she would have liked, betraying too much of how easily he had rattled her. Get a grip! she warned herself inwardly. Morgan in this mood was like some watchful predator. Show a moment of weakness and he would pounce.

'You don't need to be shown anything—you could walk round the entire place in two minutes flat.'

'Nevertheless I expect you to fulfil the agreement. Come on, Ellie,' he cajoled, his voice deepening, softening, his smile an enticement in itself. 'Indulge me in this.'

For a brief second Ellie actually had to close her eyes against the appeal of his voice that curled around her senses like a plume of warm smoke, soft as a caress. She had never been able to resist him when he'd switched on the charm like this, and to her horror she found that she still couldn't.

'Very well, then...'

Reaching back into her past, she dragged out from some hidden corner the image of the woman she had once been. The Eleanor Thornton who had been second in command of a large, profitable secretarial agency. The Eleanor Thornton that Morgan had first met.

Adopting a tone of voice that was all control, all businesslike and nothing more, she even managed to flash a swift and obviously insincere smile into his watchful face.

'If you'll just come this way, I'll show you where everything is. And perhaps you'd like to know a little bit about the area too.'

This was better; she was in the swing of things now. After all, she had done this many times before. Meadow Cottage had been occupied almost every week since Easter, and Ellie had usually been the one to greet the new tenants.

'Watch the floor here,' she said when, after unlocking the door, she made her way into the narrow hall. 'It's a little uneven. As you will have seen in the brochure, Meadow Cottage was formerly one of the farm's cowsheds, and these stone flags formed part of the original flooring.'

Her voice was perfectly steady as she went into the well-worn patter she had used so often before, but her control over the rest of her body wasn't quite so complete. When a struggle with the slightly stiff door brought him to her side to help her, the brush of his tall, strong body against her own in the constricted, confined space sent her senses into overdrive.

He still wore the same aftershave that had been a favourite when they had been together; one that she had bought for him for the only Christmas and birthday they had shared. Just the scent of it was like an instant shot of memory, jolting her back in time to those gentler, happier days.

But underneath the evocative cologne was the subtler, more intensely personal scent of his body that stabbed straight to her heart as it stirred up the waters of the past, bringing to the surface the bitter-sweet recollection of how it had felt to lie in bed with him, her head pillowed on the strength of his shoulder, breathing in the clean, musky scent of his skin.

At once all her familiar spiel deserted her. Her head was buzzing, her senses stirring in a disturbingly primitive way. For a moment the memories that gripped her were so powerful, so real that her eyes burned with bitter tears and she had to blink furiously to drive them back.

'The kitchen...' was all she could manage, gritting her teeth against the sting of irony in his murmured, 'Obviously.'

From then onwards all she wanted to do was to get the job done as quickly as possible. Not giving him time to look around, she marched him to the next door, opening it briefly.

'The sitting room... The second bedroom is up there...'

A wave of her hand indicated the small gallery above the sitting room where a neat bedroom nestled under the eaves.

'The bathroom is down here... And the main bedroom directly opposite. You can get milk and eggs from the farm—everything else from the store in the village, and they'll cash a cheque for you in an emergency. I'm afraid there isn't a bank anywhere nearer than St Austell. We provide fresh linen and towels on Mondays.'

There, she was done! Surely now he had to let her go.

'Is there anything else?'

'Just a couple of things. But why don't we discuss them over coffee?'

'No, thanks,' Ellie managed through teeth gritted against the urge to scream in frustration. 'I have other things to do.'

'And I have things I want to discuss.'

Blatantly ignoring her protest, he turned and headed back down the white-walled corridor to the kitchen, leaving her with no option but to follow him.

'Morgan, I don't have time for coffee. I have to work...'

The need for her daughter was like an ache in her heart, a hunger that no food could possibly assuage.

'Work?'

The look he directed at her burned with frank scepticism.

'You working on a farm—that's not at all what I'd have expected from the elegant Ms Thornton.'

'I told you, I'm not the same person any more. I've changed a lot in the past eighteen months.'

'So I see.'

His tone was a slow drawl and those brilliant eyes swept over her in a deliberately insolent assessment. She couldn't miss the way that sapphire gaze lingered around the fullness of her breasts, the curves of her hips in the close-fitting skirt.

As a result of her pregnancy she had filled out noticeably, so that her shape was definitely more womanly when contrasted with her slenderness when they had been together. And Morgan, who had known her body with the intimacy of a lover, couldn't be unaware of those changes either.

'So I see,' he repeated, and there was no mistaking the disturbingly sensual note on the words.

She knew that purring tone of voice. Knew only too well what it implied. She had heard it often enough when they had lived together. Then it had made her heart leap in anticipation, had set her body tingling in uncontrolled response. Just to hear her name spoken in that huskily appreciative way had been like a subtle form of foreplay, telling her instantly what was in his mind, and triggering off the same heated longings in her own.

But hearing it now shocked her rigid. Foolishly, naively perhaps, she had expected that the feelings Morgan had once had for her, *every* type of feeling, would have died, starved into non-existence by eighteen months of lack of nourishment. But there was no mistaking the heated desire that now flared in the brilliance of his eyes, the instant response that made his pupils so huge and dark.

'Country life obviously suits you. You're looking really well.'

'I'm happy here.'

She had learned how to be happy but it hadn't come easily to her. At first she had felt as if half of her soul had been cut away and it had only been the need to care for the baby growing in her womb that had kept her going.

'So why don't you make that coffee while I unload the car and then you can tell me all about it?'

Ellie's breath hissed in through her teeth in a sound of exasperation.

'Morgan, what part of what I said did you not understand? I don't have time for this...'

But she was speaking to empty air. Morgan had already opened the door and gone out to the car. When she hurried after him it was to find that he'd opened the boot and was pulling a case from it.

'Why won't you listen to me? I can't stay! Nan's expecting me—she'll be wondering where I am.'

'I never thought of Marion as a slave-driver.'

He was coming back to the door again now, a suitcase in either hand so that Ellie had to flatten herself against the wall to let him past.

'And I'm sure she'll understand that you and I will need to spend a little time getting reacquainted.'

'We're not going to get reacquainted or *re* anything.'

Her words would have more emphasis if she didn't have to keep trotting after him, forcing her shorter legs to keep up with the long, swift strides that took him through the cottage and into the ground-floor bedroom in the space of a few seconds.

'I told you—the only reason I'm here is because you're a guest and it's part of my duties to make sure you're settled in.'

'And to arrange the other services you'll provide,' Morgan returned sharply, dumping the cases on the floor and heading back to the car again.

'Services?'

It was a squawk of panic, both at the thought of just what he might have in mind and because he had come to an abrupt halt, whirling round to face her so that she had to screech to a stop herself, narrowly avoiding slamming straight into his chest.

'I was given to understand by Mr Knightley that you provided a cleaning service.'

'Well, yes…yes, we do. But surely—'

'And some meals?'

'Yes—for long-stay guests we can provide an evening meal…'

Too late she saw just where his thoughts were heading.

'Oh, no! No way! I'm not—'

'But it's in the contract.'

Anyone else might only have heard the gentle reminder in his comment but, knowing Morgan as she did, Ellie was hypersensitive to the ominous undertone that threaded darkly through the words.

'I know it's in the contract, but surely now you can't expect us to keep to it.'

'Why not?'

'Well—isn't it obvious? I mean, you won't want *me* round the house every day.'

'Won't I?' Morgan's expression gave nothing away. 'As a matter of fact I think it could work very well. You know my ways—know not to move papers, the crazy hours I work, the food I like. You'd be less likely to disturb me than a stranger.'

'But Dee—the housekeeper—she usually…'

Her voice failed her as she saw the adamant shake of his dark head.

'Not Dee,' he stated in a voice that brooked no further argument. 'I want you, angel. You and no one else.'

'I won't do it.'

For one thing she couldn't be away from Rosie that long—and she certainly didn't plan on bringing her little daughter along to the cottage with her. And for another, she already felt emotionally mangled after barely half an hour in Morgan's presence. There was no way she could cope with the prospect of seeing him for long periods of time, day after day.

'You'll have to find someone else.'

'I don't want anyone else.'

The blue eyes were like shards of ice, hard and implacable. Past experience told her that arguing with Morgan at times like this was like banging her head hard against a brick wall; that she was only hurting herself by continuing, but she couldn't give in.

'What is this? Some sort of power game? A way of getting back at me for leaving you? Do you get some sort of perverse pleasure out of the prospect of seeing me skivvying for you?'

'Is the idea of doing a few hours' simple housework so humiliating?' Morgan shot back at her.

Not for anyone else. But working for Morgan—working *with* Morgan was quite a different prospect. Where he was concerned nothing was 'simple' at all.

'I don't find it in the least humiliating—normally! Actually, I quite enjoy it. And as a matter of fact, the additional services were my idea. I suggested we put them…'

'In the contract,' Morgan finished for her with grim satisfaction when, seeing how her foolish outburst had trapped her, she let the sentence trail off weakly. 'Believe me, Ellie, I intend to keep you to every letter of every word of that agreement. There's no way I'm going to let you run out on this.'

He didn't add the words 'as you did before', but they were there at the back of what he was saying, implied by his scathing tone and the black, burning look that seared over her skin.

'I didn't "run out"!' she protested. 'I explained.'

'Oh, yeah.'

The harshness of his tone slashed into her heart like a savage sword.

'You said that things had changed. You "didn't feel the same way any more".'

Hearing the words flung at her so brutally, Ellie could only wince inwardly at the realisation of how inadequate they sounded.

But she couldn't possibly have told the truth. And even to protect her unborn child she couldn't have told Morgan that she no longer loved him.

'Well, my feelings had changed—*I'd* changed!'

Changed in the most fundamental way it was possible for a woman to do so. She had become pregnant and, knowing how he would react to that one basic fact, she had seen leaving him as the only course open to her.

'You certainly had.'

Morgan leaned back against the wall, arms folded across the width of his chest, eyeing her with bleak cynicism.

'If I'd been a betting man, angel, I'd have put money on the fact that we had something special...'

'Well, you'd have been wrong.'

He would never know how much it cost her to say those words. Because she too had thought they had had 'something special' and she had dreamed of it staying that way. Of it growing and flowering into the sort of relationship you could build a lifetime upon. She had even let herself dream of marriage, maybe, one day.

But there had been one small flaw in the perfection of her love. Morgan didn't want children. He had been absolutely emphatic on that matter right from the start. Had warned her that if she hadn't been able to cope with the idea then he'd been prepared to break it off now, before either of them had got in too deep.

But Ellie had already been in too deep. She had told herself she could manage—that Morgan himself was enough for her. And he had been enough—until the day she had realised that an accident had happened and that in spite of her precautions she was going to have a baby.

Ellie came back into the present with a jolt, and, looking deep into those inimical blue eyes, she shivered involuntarily, fearful of the cold antipathy she could see in their depths.

'Nothing stays the same for ever,' she managed, ruthlessly suppressing her voice's tendency to wobble revealingly.

'Nothing stays the same...' Morgan echoed viciously. 'How true. Nothing—not even the protestations of undying love, the vows of eternal faithfulness, the declarations that you had never felt this way before, would never feel it again. How long did it last, my angel? Ten months? A year?'

'Oh, stop it!'

Ellie longed to lift her hands and clap them over her ears, anything to drown out the brutal litany of scorn he was subjecting her to.

'I never thought—I... I'm sorry...' she finished miserably, knowing she had to say it, even though it was hopelessly inadequate and far, far too late. 'I'm really sorry. If I could say anything—'

'No!' Morgan cut in harshly. 'Don't! Don't say anything—and *don't* say that you're sorry—because I'm not! I was angry when you left—true. I was even a little hurt at the thought that you could discard me so easily, move on to someone else. But when I calmed down and started thinking rationally again, I realised that in fact you'd done me one hell of a favour.'

'A favour?'

'Yeah, a favour. I was close to making the biggest mistake of my life with you.'

He shook his head as if in despair at his own foolishness.

'Something I would have regretted for as long as I lived. But by leaving when you did, you saved me from that. Really, instead of reproaching you, I reckon I should thank you.'

'Don't bother!' Ellie snapped, unable to take any more.

For the first time she admitted to herself that she had come here with a tiny thread of a weak, foolish hope in her heart. Hopes of a reconciliation, of finding that Morgan, too, had suffered from their time apart, and so might be prepared to rethink his feeling about children. But his comments had not only taken that pathetic hope away from her, they had crushed it into tiny, irreparable pieces, impossible ever to put together again.

'Well, at least you won't expect me to stay after—'

'Oh, but I do,' Morgan cut in sharply. 'In fact, now I want that coffee more than ever.'

'Well, you can just go on wanting! I'm finished here, I—'

'But *I* haven't finished with *you*,' Morgan came back at her with deadly quietness. 'There are things we still have to talk about.'

He pushed himself away from the wall, straightening up lazily.

'Make the coffee, Ellie,' he said and it was a command, not a request.

CHAPTER THREE

FOR a moment Morgan thought he'd lost her.

He knew that look of old. The set jaw, the compressed mouth, the mutinous glare that declared only too clearly that Ellie was having none of whatever she thought he was suggesting.

This was Ellie at her most stubborn, and, strangely enough, it was seeing her in this mood that reached out and stabbed him in the heart, when he least expected it to.

This was the Ellie who had most infuriated him when they'd been together. The woman who could set against something, however small, and turn it into a battle, one she had no intention of letting him win. There had never been any chance of wearing her down when she'd been like this. In fact there had only ever been one approach that had a chance of winning her round.

So he used it.

'Please…' he added softly, pitching his voice at a very different level.

She wasn't going to give in that easily, it was clear. Just one swift, stunned blink of those amazing eyes showed any sort of response, making Morgan wonder exactly why he was so set on having her stay when quite clearly she would rather be anywhere but here.

But perhaps that was the whole point. Whatever was bugging her, it was pretty damn important to her. And the more she seemed determined not to let any hint of it drop, the more he wanted to know what it was.

'Ellie…'

27

He pushed one long-fingered hand through his ebony hair, raking it back from his face with a sigh.

'I've been driving for hours and I really could murder for a coffee.'

He did look tired, Ellie admitted to herself reluctantly. Typical Morgan. When he was working, or concentrating on anything, he forgot about minor practicalities like food or drink.

'What are you afraid of if you stay?' Morgan questioned softly.

'Nothing.' It didn't sound at all convincing. 'What on earth makes you think that I'm *afraid*?'

That was better. She might even believe herself now. But she knew only too well what she was afraid of—and with good reason. She just couldn't bring herself to admit it.

'Just one cup of coffee,' she growled reluctantly, risking a swift glance at his face and immediately wishing she hadn't as she was rewarded with the sort of wide, flashing smile that would have melted rock, never mind her weak, foolish heart.

'You're an angel.'

'It will only be instant...'

Desperately she tried to claw back some of the ground she had surrendered.

'Fine!'

He punctured her sense of triumph quickly and easily, tossing the response over his shoulder as he headed back out to the car.

Struggling to keep her mind blank, Ellie moved to fill and switch on the kettle. One cup of coffee wouldn't take very long. She'd be on her way in no time.

At least she didn't have to worry about Rosie. Even if the little girl had woken from her nap, she would have Nan and Dee to take care of her. She'd known both women all her short life and had had them wrapped round one small, chubby finger since the day she'd been born.

'You couldn't rustle up a sandwich or something as well, could you?'

Morgan dropped a cardboard box of groceries on the kitchen table beside her, startling her out of her thoughts.

'There's bread and cheese in there somewhere.'

'When did you last eat?'

It wouldn't be held back, the sense of exasperation painfully familiar.

He paused briefly to consider, then shrugged his broad shoulders.

'Don't know.'

He was too close, that evocative scent setting her nerves prickling again. The sun slanting in through the kitchen window gleamed on hair of ebony silk, highlighting sapphire eyes behind a fringe of outrageously thick dark lashes. Narrow hips in snug fitting denim rested casually against the side of the table, and he had rolled up his sleeves revealing tanned and muscular forearms, lightly covered in soft dark hair.

'Didn't want to waste time stopping. And you know what motorway services are like.'

And she knew what Morgan was like. Motorway services, with his best-sellers on display in the shops, meant the possibility of being recognised, something he avoided like the plague. Ellie bit down hard on her lip as she struggled with the twist of pain in her heart that came with yet another reminder of just how well she had once known this man.

'But a sandwich would be very welcome…and if you could slice up some tomatoes as well…'

'What did your last servant die of?' Ellie flung after him, his laughter in response infuriating her further.

But she was only protesting to save face, she knew. She would do it, dammit. She would make him his coffee and his sandwich not just because she felt she had no option. She couldn't even deceive herself with the thought that she would do the same for any new guest who had had a long journey.

She would do it because she couldn't help herself. Because she could no longer deny herself the opportunity to do this small thing for this man who had once meant all the world to her. Sighing, she rooted in the box, pulled out bread, cheese.

It was as she was slicing into the crisp crust of the loaf that memory struck, hard and sharp, stilling her hand and holding her frozen, staring straight ahead with sightless, unfocussed eyes.

It had been—what?—over two years ago. A warm June evening, not unlike today. The night she had moved to Morgan's London apartment following his suggestion that she come and live with him. Of course, she hadn't hesitated. She'd been crazily out of her mind with love, her 'Yes' had been out of her mouth almost before he'd finished asking, and she had moved in the very next day.

Then, as now, Morgan had directed her into the kitchen, suggesting she prepare something for them to eat while he unloaded her belongings from the car.

The knife shook in Ellie's hand, tears stinging cruelly as she recalled how he had whistled as he'd worked. How each time he had passed her he had flashed that wide, devastating smile that had turned her insides to molten liquid, and snatched a kiss or simply let his hands trail along her back, her shoulders, her hair. It was if he hadn't been able to keep his hands off her and had had to keep reassuring himself that she'd been there.

And then, when everything had been unloaded, he had come up behind her, sliding strong, warm arms around her slim waist, resting his head on her shoulder, his breath warm against her cheek...

This had been a mistake, Morgan told himself as he slammed the now-empty boot of the car shut and turned to the last box that still lay on the back seat of the Alfa Romeo. One hell of a stupid mistake.

It was no wonder that he'd had a sense of *déjà vu*. No wonder that it seemed as if he'd lived through this before. It was almost an exact replay of the day that Ellie had first moved in with him.

'Oh, hell!'

Forgetting the box for a moment, he rested his arms on the sun-warmed top of the car, his chin supported on one hand as he let the memories roll over him.

He'd never been so happy. Or so scared. Never in all his twenty-eight years had he known a feeling like it. He still couldn't actually believe that he'd made the move, spoken the words that he'd been sure he'd never say to anyone.

Or that she had agreed.

He hadn't known that he was going to say anything. No rational thought, no careful preparation had come into his head. One moment he'd been lying there, his heart still thudding, his skin still slick with sweat after the blazing passion of their lovemaking, the next he had turned and looked into her face and just *known*.

But the feeling had been still too new, too delicate, to share with anyone, even Ellie. Ellie who'd declared 'I love you' as easily as breathing, who'd seemed to have no fear, no doubts.

And so he'd gone for the casual approach.

'I think, after that, saying goodnight and going home alone has definitely lost its appeal. How do you feel about making this into a—more logical arrangement?'

'Coffee's ready!'

Ellie's call from the kitchen splintered his memories, bringing his head up sharply, reminding him where he was.

It was just as well he'd held back on his true feelings, he

reflected cynically as he forced his mind back on to the present and, collecting the last box, headed inside once more. Ellie's 'love', so carelessly given, had been just as easily taken away again. They had had perhaps eleven months before he had felt her attention drifting and barely two weeks after that she had told him she was leaving.

'Is that the last one?'

Ellie was buttering bread, her attention fixed on what she was doing, and she glanced up casually as he came in.

'Just dump it somewhere and come and get your coffee while it's hot. Not that dump is the appropriate word,' she added as her eyes focussed on what he was carrying. 'That's a laptop, isn't it?'

'The newest, state-of-the-art, portable wonder machine.' Morgan nodded, concentrating unnecessarily hard on placing the box carefully on the sideboard while he got his thoughts back under control. 'It does everything I want of it. If I could just get it to create plots for me as well, then it would be perfect.'

He was talking to distract himself, he knew. He should never have let himself remember what it felt like to make love to her. Never have recalled the blazing desire, the pounding of his blood in his veins, the hungry kisses and even hungrier caresses. Just to think of them made his body tighten, setting up an ache that left him fighting for control.

'You've made enough sandwiches to feed an army.' He struggled to keep the conversation light.

'Self-defence,' Ellie returned, concentrating fiercely on laying pieces of tomato on top of the thinly sliced cheese. 'I know what your temper's like when you're hungry—it's one thing about you that I have most definitely not missed.'

'So there are things that you *do* miss?'

He couldn't stop himself from moving closer, had to clench his hands tight in the pockets of his jeans so as to resist the temptation to touch. A shining golden strand of

her hair had fallen forward over her cheek and his fingers
itched to smooth it back, tangle in the rest of the silken
weight.

'Oh, yes...'

Did he have to come so close? Every nerve in her body
sang with tension, tight as the strings of a harp, and the race
of her heart made it a struggle to breathe.

'I miss the tip that your office turns into when you are
working. The way you are perfectly capable of forgetting
about the practicalities of life and existing on nothing but
endless mugs of coffee. I miss the impossible hours you
work. The way you forget about appointments, social com-
mitments, invitations...'

'You obviously have very fond memories!' Morgan put
in wryly.

Lord, but she smelled good. A mixture of roses and sun-
shine and the private, sweet scent of her skin. It drew her
to him as if her body were a powerful magnet and his just
a powerless needle, tugged into her gentle but irresistible
force field.

'Leave me some self-respect.'

His plea was accompanied by such a ruefully pained expression that the boyish appeal of it twisted sharply in
Ellie's heart. Was it just her imagination or had he moved
even closer?

'I didn't expect such a demolition job on my character.'

Black pepper, Ellie told herself, forcing her thoughts onto
practical matters. Morgan loved black pepper on tomatoes.

Reaching for the pepper mill, she twisted the top fiercely,
then stilled abruptly as the movement brought her into contact with Morgan's right arm, the soft brush against the
warmth of his skin sending a searing electric spark of response right down to her toes until they curled inside her
shoes.

'Is there anything else you miss?'

His hand snaked out and snatched up one of the ripe, moist slices of tomato speckled with spicy flecks of black pepper and he bit into it appreciatively, his teeth very white and strong.

'Yes,' Ellie managed in a voice that sounded rusty and raw as if it hadn't been used for some time. 'I miss the way you steal food when I'm preparing it and you can't wait... Stop it!'

He'd reached for another segment of the fruit, but this time she was ready for him. This time she moved as quickly as he had, giving the back of his hand a gentle slap before closing her fingers around his wrist to still it.

And froze.

Her heart was beating high up in her throat. Her fingers were clenched over the hard bones, feeling the powerful muscles tighten suddenly, then relax again, but still holding a tension that communicated itself silently to her quivering sense. Unable to control herself, she drew in one swift, shuddering breath and let it go again on a ragged sigh.

Behind her, Morgan shifted slightly, coming so close that she could feel the warmth of his long body all the way down her back.

'Ellie,' he said softly, and his voice sounded as raw and husky as hers had just a moment before so that she had to close her eyes against the sharp tug of its appeal to her already heightened senses.

'Morgan...' She tried to protest, but either her voice failed her and he didn't hear or he heard and deliberately ignored it, bringing his head down so that he could whisper in her ear, the heat of his breath feathering against her skin.

'Do you know what I miss about you, angel?'

'No...'

Even she didn't know if she meant to encourage him to go on or quite the opposite. But whatever was in her mind, the word had no effect. Morgan didn't even pause to listen but continued inexorably.

'I miss the feel of your hair...'

His cheek rested against the blonde strands, soft as a caress.

'The scent of your skin. I miss the sound of your breath, your voice, your heartbeat next to mine. I miss the softness of your flesh underneath my fingertips.'

With his free hand he traced a delicate, tantalising path along the side of her cheek and down the slender line of her throat, pausing briefly to rest on the point at the base of her neck where her pulse leapt and throbbed in heady, drumming response.

'Morgan...'

The knife she was holding fell from Ellie's loosened grasp to land with a clatter on the table-top and the hand that held his shifted slightly, moving from restraint to a softer embrace. The pad of her thumb moved over the heated satin of his skin, tracing out an enticing pattern that brought a murmur of response from his throat.

'I miss the taste of you on my lips, in my mouth...'

His lips had replaced the touch of his hands, following the same path down her face, kissing her forehead, her temple, her closed eyelid, the fine line of her cheekbone. With the heat of response flooding through her, Ellie felt her whole body melt, becoming pliant as wax. With a soft murmur she let her head fall against his shoulder, releasing his hand, no longer able to keep hold of it.

Immediately his newly free arm came round her, fastening about her waist and pulling her tight against him. She welcomed the support of his strength, knowing that her own had deserted her, that she was incapable of holding herself upright.

'The feel of your breasts in my hands...'

Suiting actions to the words, he slid his hands upward,

cupping her breasts in the heat of his palms, his thumbs stroking over the hardening points of her nipples. Against her back, she could feel the potent evidence of his desire, hot and swollen and forceful, and the memories it roused in her made her senses swim.

His fingers were busy with the buttons on her blouse now, easing them swiftly and efficiently from their fastenings, letting the soft white cotton ease apart. One hand slipped inside the white lacy cup of the bra underneath, drawing a shuddering sigh of response as she felt its caress against the smooth slope of her breast.

'Morgan!'

It was a choking cry of delight, of appeal, of surrender all in one, and she whirled round in the confining hold of his arms and crushed the aching tips of her breasts against his chest. Her arms went up around his neck, her fingers lacing in the darkness of his hair, and she drew his head down urgently to hers.

His kiss felt like coming home. Hard and demanding, it pressed her lips open to the hungry invasion of his tongue, his hands twisting in her hair, fingers clenching around her skull, bringing her even closer to him.

Heavy waves of desire rolled over her, hot and thick and hungry, swamping her mind and driving away almost all coherent thought. All coherent thought but one. Because now the word that she had dodged away from, the word she had feared, had been unable to face since she had known she would have to see him again, was the only thing that was clear inside her thoughts. Over and over it repeated, again and again, swirling round the inside of her skull like a litany of need.

Love. That was the word she had been avoiding; the word she couldn't bring herself to consider. It meant too much, hurt too much, laid her open to too much danger.

But now she knew she couldn't avoid it any longer. She

still loved Morgan, always had loved him, would always love him. That was the cruellest irony of their situation. She had been forced into making him believe that she no longer loved him, when in fact nothing could be further from the truth. She loved this man more than all the world, and only the love of one other human being, her child, could ever have forced her from his side.

But now Morgan was back. His arms were round her, his lips on hers. She could see the passion in his darkened eyes, the flare of colour on the carved cheekbones, and she knew there was no way she could deny herself this. Her hands shook with the pent-up need of long months apart, making her fumble with buttons on his shirt in her haste to touch him. Really touch him. To feel the heat and smoothness of his skin under her urgent fingertips.

'Easy, angel...' Morgan murmured, his voice thickened by a matching desire, but she shook her head frantically, too overwhelmed, too lost in sensation to heed.

At last she reached her goal, smoothing her palms over the warm flesh, the springing dark hairs with a deep sigh of satisfaction. She wanted to touch him everywhere, couldn't get enough of him.

'Morgan...Morgan...'

She muttered his name restlessly, feverishly, the two syllables the only sound her mouth could form in between the hungrily snatched kisses as she added the unique taste of his skin to the thousand other sensations that were bombarding her awareness.

'Ellie!'

On a groan of surrender Morgan gave up all attempt to speak and swept her up into his arms. Shouldering open the door, he took her through the small living room, down the corridor, and into the ground floor bedroom. One of his cases still lay where he had dumped it on the unmade bed, but he violently kicked it aside, almost falling onto the mattress, taking Ellie with him.

With more haste than gentleness he rushed her shirt and the delicate bra underneath it from her yearning body, and now it was his turn to use her name as a form of incantation, an expression of longing that could not be held back.

'Ellie…Ellie…' he muttered over and over, hands twisting in her tumbled hair, smoothing over her skin, sliding under her breasts, lifting them to the heated attentions of his lips.

The first, almost gentle kisses on the creamy slopes soon changed in the space of a frantic heartbeat to hungrier, more passionate caresses. The sharp tug of his mouth on one achingly sensitive nipple made Ellie cry out in shock and delight, her body writhing in uncontrolled response to the stinging pleasure. Pushing aside his loosened shirt, her fingers clenched over the powerful bones of his shoulders, closing over hard muscle, feeling it bunch and move under her grip.

'I want you…I want you…'

She could hardly believe it was her own voice she heard, it sounded so rough and raw. But she seemed to have lost control of her tongue and the muttered plea escaped of its own volition.

'You'll have me, angel…' was Morgan's breathless, laughter-shaken response. 'Just as soon as I can get rid of these—these damn clothes!'

The red skirt was too tight, the fastening too time consuming for his hunger and, abandoning with a rough, exasperated curse the attempt to open it, he reached for the hem instead, pushing it violently up over the slender length of her legs, to bunch in crumpled disorder around her waist.

Because of the warmth of the summer, she wore no tights or stockings and the small scrap of satin and lace that was the only delicate barrier to his demanding hands was soon discarded, tossed aside without a care for where it landed.

'You too...' Ellie muttered, fingers made clumsy with need as she tugged at the buckle of his belt, yanking it loose.

He helped her with the single button underneath. She heard the faint rasp of the zip sliding down and caught her breath in sharp anticipation. It felt as if a hungry fire blazed deep inside her, sending rivulets of heat out through every nerve, pulsing between her legs, and she couldn't wait for the thrusting force of his possession to ease the yearning ache.

But something had changed. Above her, Morgan had stilled, his face changing suddenly. His expression darkened and he looked deep into her passion-glazed eyes, frowning as he searched for some answer there.

'Ellie—we can't...'

Disappointment and the savage bite of frustrated need scythed through her like a heated sword. Totally at the mercy of her clamouring body, she turned a bruise-dark gaze on his hard, set face.

'Yes, we can! We *can*!' she protested as, unbelievingly, she saw him shake his head. 'Morgan!'

'Answer me one question, Ellie. Are you protected? Are you on the pill or...?'

If he had slapped her brutally in the face he couldn't have brought her out of the heady delirium faster or more cruelly. Ellie could only stare at him in shocked distress until, slowly and unwillingly, her mind began to realise just what he had said and why.

Are you protected? Oh, she knew that question of old. Knew how he could express it in a way that sounded like concern for her and for her alone. But she knew the truth. And the truth was that Morgan Stafford had made it plain that he had never wanted children. Not with her, not with anyone.

'No...' she managed shakily, and the look on his face, the shock in those deep blue eyes said it all.

Already he was withdrawing from her, moving back, putting a distance that was more than physical between them. One that tore at her heart with the pain of both the present and a past when this had divided them so savagely.

Are you protected? He wanted to protect himself against the possibility of a child he didn't want being created as a result of their lovemaking.

But the truth was that it was already too late. Almost twenty months before, the protection he so valued had failed. Morgan didn't know it but he already had a daughter. But a daughter he would never want, never acknowledge. And because of that there could never be any future for the two of them.

CHAPTER FOUR

'GET off me!'

The change was so sudden, so stunning that for a second or two Morgan could almost believe another woman had taken Ellie's place.

Gone was the willingly wanton bedmate he had anticipated, and in her place was a furiously distant iceberg, one whose golden eyes sparked with furious rejection where before he had seen burning hunger and a passion to match his own. It was so totally unexpected that he actually laughed.

'I said, get off me!'

This time the cold command was accompanied by a threatening movement of one leg, her knee coming up with such obviously ominous intent that any man would very rapidly think twice about remaining in the danger zone.

Not being prepared to take the risk, he moved swiftly, jackknifing off the bed. The bite of the denim shirt into his arms reminded him of the way Ellie had pushed it down from his shoulders, imprisoning him. With an angry movement he shrugged it back into position again just as Ellie twisted herself off the bed, frantically pushing at the bunched and crumpled skirt to cover herself.

'Just what the hell is going on here?' he demanded, matching her fury with his own, an aggrieved sense of injustice combining with a hard ache of frustration with explosive results. 'When I show consideration for the possible consequences of my—our—actions, I don't expect to be turned on as if I've tried to force myself on you.'

When he'd shown *consideration*! Ellie's mind nearly

41

blew a fuse at the thought. She knew damn well that he was not *considering* her in the slightest!

All he wanted was to avoid the encumbrance of a child. If she needed any further evidence that her decision not to tell him about Rosie had been the right one, it was staring her in the face. In fact her grandmother had been the only person she had told the truth about Rosie's father, and that was the way she wanted it to stay.

'Or were you just leading me on, playing some nasty little game?'

'No! Oh, no!'

But she had to say something to explain her behaviour. To distract him from the dangerous path his thoughts were taking.

'You're forgetting something,' she blustered nervously, backing away from the glare he turned on her.

'And what, precisely, am I forgetting, my angel?'

'Not what—*who*. You're forgetting about Pete.'

'Pete!'

He spat the name out as if it were an obscenity. To her horror all the fire seemed to have died out of his eyes, replaced by an icy cold that seemed to flay a layer of skin from her body, leaving her agonisingly exposed and desperately vulnerable.

Suddenly terribly aware of the fact that she was only half dressed, the crumpled skirt all that covered her, she turned wide desperate eyes to hunt for her missing clothing. Her bra seemed to have disappeared completely and her white blouse lay just inches from Morgan's feet. No matter how urgently she longed to pick it up and pull it on, she didn't dare risk moving to retrieve it. Not while he was in this mood. So instead she had to content herself with crossing her arms across her exposed breasts in order to provide an inadequate form of protection.

'Pete Bedford,' Morgan repeated with ominous quietness. 'And just what has he to do with this?'

Something was wrong here. He'd been told that Pete Bedford was no longer in the picture. The realisation that the other man was still part of Ellie's life was like a kick in the teeth, combining with the savage nag of a frustrated libido to leave him incapable of thinking straight.

'Isn't it obvious? I—couldn't possibly sleep with you b-because of Pete...' she managed clumsily.

Something in what she'd said had surprised him. His dark head went back sharply, blue eyes narrowing in swift appraisal.

'But I thought that you two were no longer an item.'

There it was again. The suggestion—more than a suggestion—that Morgan was not here by chance but that he had somehow found out exactly where she was and had come here forewarned—and forearmed—by knowledge about her circumstances.

'Of course he's in the picture! He's headmaster of a school in Truro.'

Morgan took a moment to absorb that fact.

'I see,' he said at last. 'And I presume that you suddenly had a belated attack of conscience because it would mean being unfaithful to dear Pete.'

'It wasn't *belated*! And I'll tell you this whether you believe it or not—I have never—*never*—been unfaithful to any man while we were still officially together.'

'You came pretty close to it a moment ago. I'd say your second thoughts came just that bit too late to leave you totally innocent of all charges. Or are you trying to claim that I forced you?'

'I wouldn't dare.'

Morgan nodded his grim satisfaction.

'At least you have the honesty to admit to the truth. I've never forced a woman in my life.'

'Of course not!'

It was impossible to hide her pain, though she tried to mask it behind a show of scorn that she hoped was convincing.

'I suppose you believe you're so totally irresistible that no woman can resist you!'

Images she didn't want to face were filling her mind. Images of a string of newspaper reports that she had seen in the time they had been apart.

'But then of course you have the evidence of all those starlets and models to support you. Who was it last month, Morgan? Kitty Spencer? And the month before that? Macy Renton?'

A dangerous scowl creased Morgan's straight black brows and he pulled the sides of his gaping shirt together, fastening it swiftly with brusque, aggressive movements that spoke eloquently of the feelings he was holding back.

'You shouldn't believe everything you read in the papers,' he snarled.

'Oh, so nothing of what was reported is true?' Her eyebrows shot up in cynical query and scepticism dripped from her voice.

The scowl darkened, his strong jaw tightening aggressively.

'Not nothing,' he snarled.

He wasn't proud of the way he'd behaved during the first month or so after Ellie had left him. Wasn't proud of the lengths he'd gone to to fill the emptiness she'd left behind, the women with whom he'd tried to forget her. He'd tried to go back to the sort of life he'd lived before Ellie only to find that he had moved further away from it than he'd ever dreamed.

None of it had worked. All that had happened was that he'd managed a few hours of oblivion, but the morning had always come. He'd always had to face reality again, and reality had meant the dreadful irony of knowing that now he'd been free to do whatever he wanted with his future—but that freedom and that future had meant nothing without this one woman. A woman who had turned his life upside down, changed his perspective on everything, and then walked out, leaving behind an empty hole he'd found impossible to fill.

'But at least any women I had a relationship with were free to be with me. They weren't committed to anyone else, emotionally or otherwise.'

He was pushing his shirt into the waistband of his jeans as he spoke, the brisk efficiency of his movements as he fastened the zip, buckled his belt, expressing forcefully the distance that had now come between them.

'Unlike you and your precious Pete. So what is it, my angel? Are you and your headmaster a couple or not? Or is your new man not the lover you thought he was?'

'How dare you?' Ellie threw the words into his cold face, amber eyes burning gold with fury. 'Pete has been very kind to me.'

'Oh, yes, and we both know how "kind" he's been. But perhaps that's the problem. Perhaps you don't want "kind" any more. Perhaps it doesn't satisfy you, and you're looking for something a little different—something more exciting?'

'Well, if I was, then it wouldn't be with you!'

'No?'

Sceptical ice-blue eyes went to the bed, drifted over to the suitcase he had kicked aside so violently, and then came back to her flushed and indignant face.

'No?' he questioned again on a new and very different note, one eyebrow drifting upwards in cynical query.

'Excitement wasn't the word for that!' Ellie injected every ounce of contempt she could manage into her tone. 'It was more like a form of masochism—an exorcism of any lingering delusions I might have had about you.'

'Believe me, angel,' Morgan drawled with silky menace, 'the feeling is entirely mutual. Like I said, I very nearly made the biggest mistake of my life.'

And he'd been hers, Ellie reflected bitterly. The worst mistake she had ever made in her life had been allowing herself to love him. Not that there had been any choice in the matter. She had been out of her depth almost from the very first moment she had met him. And nothing that had happened had done anything to change that.

'So at least we both know exactly where we stand,' she stated, somehow managing to make herself sound every bit as cold and uninvolved as he had done. All she wanted now was to get away from here as quickly and quietly as she possibly could. 'Would you mind passing me my blouse? I'd like to get dressed.'

Morgan stooped, picked up the discarded shirt and tossed it disdainfully in her direction. Ellie just caught it and, pointedly ignoring his hard-eyed stare, turned her back to pull it on. The brush of the soft cotton over her sensitised skin, the still-aching peaks of her breasts, was a new form of torture, but she gritted her teeth and ignored it, fastening the buttons with determined movements.

Clothed, at least she felt better, even if the shirt was dreadfully crumpled and must look like nothing more than a rag. Her hands awkward and unsteady, she tried to smooth down the tousled strands of her hair, knowing that her attempts were having very little effect at all as she swung round to face Morgan again.

He hadn't moved. He was still standing just feet away, tall and dark and devastating to her peace of mind, long hands resting loosely on the leather belt around his narrow waist, blue eyes hooded and watchful.

Ellie forced the polite, meaningless smile she used for really difficult customers, all lips and teeth, flashed on and off again, with nothing in the eyes at all.

'Well, I don't think there is anything more we need to discuss, so I'll leave you to settle in.'

He waited until she reached the bedroom door, until she was thinking thankfully of escape, of finally getting away and hiding somewhere, licking her wounds in peace.

'And you'll be back—when?' he enquired sardonically.

Never—if she had a choice.

'Back?'

'The "extra services",' Morgan reminded her harshly. 'Cleaning—meals…'

'Under the circumstances, I really think that you'd prefer it if Dee did your housekeeping after all.'

'No way.' It was a flat, emotionless statement but one that made it plain he had no intention of yielding or offering any concession on the point at all. 'I don't want this Dee, or your grandmother, or anyone else at all. I want *you*.'

'But *why*? Why me?'

Why? Morgan asked himself the same question even as he phrased the words, 'I want *you*', not quite sure he had actually heard himself speak them.

Why when she had made it plain that she hated him, that she wanted nothing more to do with him, was he still so determined to play the only cards he had left in order to keep her near him? Why the hell did he want an unwilling, hostile, spitting alley cat coming to the house every day to perform tasks that she clearly resented with every cell in her body?

If it came to that, why was he even considering staying when the information he had been given was so obviously at fault? Pete was clearly still the man in her life, even if it seemed that that relationship was not quite the happy-ever-after that she might once have dreamed it would be. That being the case, why didn't he just throw his cases back in the car and head out of here, not looking back? It would be safer and easier all round.

But somehow safe and easy didn't appeal. For one thing, the lingering ache of unassuaged desire reminded him that no woman had ever had the effect on him that this defiant, golden-haired, golden-eyed creature had always had just by existing. Even when she was spitting abuse at him, that soft mouth declaring rejection of everything he was, everything he said, she still excited him physically.

Just one smile, one soft glance from those stunning eyes, the movement of her hair, the scent of her skin, was enough to send his hormones into screaming overdrive, to know that he could never get enough of her. Face it, he told himself. In the past hour or so she had angered, appalled, disgusted and driven him to distraction until he had felt all the normal control he had on his thoughts and his emotions slipping out of his grasp. But he had also been more intensely *alive* than at any point in the past year and a half.

And he wanted more of it—whatever it took to get it.

So, 'Why?' he repeated, lifting his shoulders in an indifferent shrug that dismissed her objections as casually as he might brush away a buzzing fly. 'I told you. You suit me.'

'Well, it doesn't suit me!'

Ellie had had enough.

'I won't do it, Morgan! You can't make me—and don't tell me that it's in the damn contract!' she snapped when he opened his mouth, obviously intending to do exactly that. 'I don't care if it's written in letters of gold carved into tablets of stone. I *won't do it*!'

'You're prepared to break the contract?' he enquired with a mildness that Ellie knew only too well was deceptive, hiding a ruthless determination not to let her get the better of him in any way. 'Are you sure that's wise?'

'So sue me!'

High on the adrenaline her fury had created, Ellie tossed her defiance carelessly into his hard, set face.

'Do what you like! I don't care! I'm not coming back

here, for love or money! The contract didn't specify exactly *who* will come and housekeep for you so you'll just have to take what you get!'

She should never have looked into his face. Never have risked meeting his eyes. But she had done and now all she could see was how like Rosie he was physically.

Those blue, blue eyes were the ones that stared out at her from Rosie's face. The dark silky hair that had fallen forward over his broad forehead was an exact match for his daughter's hair. And the thought that if Morgan so much as knew that he had a daughter he would turn and walk away from her without a second glance was more than she could bear.

She had come to the cottage to meet him today with a tiny hope at the back of her mind that something he said or did would show that Morgan had changed. That he had rethought, or at least softened his stance on having children, so that her dream of letting Morgan and Rosie meet, of letting her beloved daughter get to know the man who was her father, might just possibly come true.

But now, looking into Morgan's cold, set face, seeing the rejection of everything she was in his eyes, she knew that that dream had no hope at all of coming true.

'I'll tell Dee to call round in the morning!' she flung at him. 'And if you don't like it—well, tough! That's the way it's going to be.'

And before he could react, before he could say another word to object or to keep her there, she had spun on her heel and was heading out of the house and away from him, as fast as she could go without actually running.

Because running would give the impression that she was afraid, and that was not what she wanted Morgan to think at all.

CHAPTER FIVE

WHERE had it all gone wrong?

Ellie pushed a peg onto the washing line with a force that expressed something of the turmoil of feeling she was experiencing and bent to pick up another clean, wet tablecloth from the basket.

When had her relationship with Morgan foundered? When had she realised that they were on opposite sides of a very high fence and that they could never, ever share the same point of view?

Because at first she had thought she could accept the way that Morgan felt. If she was honest, she had believed that his resolution never to have children had been just a temporary phase, not a real, final decision. She'd been convinced that, given time, as their relationship had grown, he would have changed his mind, that his had been just the stance of a young man, used to being single, who hadn't relished the thought of the restrictions on his freedom, the responsibilities that being a father would inevitably have brought.

Instinctively her eyes went to the spot where Rosie, in a red stretchy cotton top and shorts, sat, kicking contentedly in her pushchair and babbling to herself in her own private baby language. As her eyes met the bright blue ones of her daughter, her whole body clenched on a blaze of love for this tiny being who was as much a part of her as her own heart.

Immediately she had to drop the cloth back in the basket and move to Rosie's side. Crouching down by the pushchair, she stroked the small, dark-haired head gently, looking deep into the eyes that were a mirror image of Morgan's brilliant blue ones.

'I love you, darling! I love you so much.'

Another stream of happy babbling was the response, the baby stilling for a moment and looking into her mother's eyes in a moment of such intensity that Ellie's heart kicked sharply again, making her catch her breath.

'Oh, Rosie!' she sighed. 'If only it could have been different. If only...'

Abruptly she pulled herself up, refusing to let her thoughts travel down that path. There was no room for 'if only'. No possibility of it ever having been any other way. If there could have been she would have tried it. She would have tried anything other than make the decision that had torn her heart so dreadfully that she felt the wounds would never heal.

'I couldn't have both of you,' she said, capturing one wildly waving little fist and feeling the chubby fingers close around her own thumb. 'Morgan made that plain. So I had to choose. And you were the one who needed me most.'

It had been instant, that feeling of total communication, total love for the baby growing inside her. From the moment that she had first suspected she was pregnant she had known that she'd wanted this baby more than anything in the world. The sense of absolute devotion that had rushed through her had been emotion in its purest form, white-hot and primitive.

She would have fought anyone who had endangered her baby's life, thrown herself in front of a speeding car, an attacking predator, given her own life to protect that of the baby she'd instinctively adored without even knowing what sex it was.

'But I couldn't put right the worst problem of all, could I, sweetie?'

Tears stung Ellie's eyes as Rosie treated her to her most

brilliant, widest, almost toothless smile, leaning forward to
pat her mother's cheek with gentle enthusiasm.

In the beginning it hadn't mattered at all. She'd had her
own career, as the deputy manager of a secretarial agency,
and Morgan had been winning a reputation as a writer of
screenplays, as well as the dark, brooding thrillers that
topped the best-seller lists around the world. And at first
Ellie had been too stunned to think that he could want her,
that he could care enough to ask her to live with him, to
want to question anything else about their relationship.

By then, no force on earth could have stopped her from
falling heart and soul in love with him. She had even seen
his insistence on being ultra-careful about contraception as
an indication of the way he'd felt about her, a way of making sure that no accident had happened before she'd been
ready to think about having children.

Looking back, she had realised that she had often been
forced into interpreting his actions rather than really knowing what he'd felt. Morgan was a man who played his cards
very close to his chest, never expressing his emotions
openly.

Ellie's bronze eyes dulled and she stood, staring sight-
lessly into the distance as she recalled the first time she had
truly become aware of the gulf between her and Morgan
over one very vital subject.

They had been out to dinner with a colleague of Ellie's
from the agency and her husband. During the evening Jackie
had announced that she had just had her first pregnancy
confirmed, and from the start it had been obvious that
Morgan hadn't shared everyone else's delight.

'You could have been a little more enthusiastic!' Ellie
challenged him when they were in the car on the way home.

'About what?' Morgan's voice was tight and cold, his
attention fixed on the road ahead so that his sculpted profile

was etched, harsh and unyielding, against the darkness of the car window.

'You know what! Jackie was pregnant and she wanted everyone to celebrate with her. And all you could do was to sit and glower in your corner. I had to work really hard to cover up the way your mood clashed with everyone else's.'

'I didn't feel enthusiastic.'

'But you must have done. Anyone would be happy at the news...'

Her voice trickled away as she realised just what his silence, the tension in the long body beside her, was communicating. As she turned to glance at him he simply shook his head, the slow, emphatic movement leaving little room for doubt.

'What is this, Morgan? Are you trying to say that you're not that keen on kids?'

'I'm not *trying* to say anything—I'm telling you. And what I'm telling you is not that I'm "not keen" on kids, but that they are just not part of my life. Never have been and never will be.'

She felt as if she had been slammed hard against a brick wall, knocking herself out for a couple of seconds, so that when she came round she was still, mentally at least, seeing stars. She had never thought to raise the subject of having children with Morgan because she'd been afraid that it might seem that she was angling for marriage, something he had never suggested. While their relationship was still so new and vulnerable she had been quite frankly terrified of rocking any boats that might mean she would lose him for good.

But she had always assumed...

They were pulling up outside Morgan's house when she finally collected her thoughts enough to speak again.

'You don't mean that—you can't.'

'Can't I?'

The dark undertone in his voice warned her to leave the subject alone, but Ellie was beyond heeding the danger signal. Coming from a family of five herself, she had always wanted children, at least two, of her own, and it had never crossed her mind that her chosen partner in life might not feel the same way.

Morgan had got out of the car and was unlocking the front door. She had to hurry after him as he headed into the unlighted hall.

'Of course you don't mean it! Everyone wants kids eventually.'

'Not me.'

It was cold and clipped and utterly implacable, and his eyes, when he snapped on the light so suddenly that she blinked in shock, were as cold and bleak as a midnight sky in winter.

'Let's get something straight, Ellie. I never intend to become a father. There's no place in my life for children and there never will be. If you can't accept that, then we'd better call a halt right here and now.'

'You don't...'

But then, seeing the look of withdrawal on Morgan's face, the distance that he had somehow put between them without ever having moved an inch, she recognised the true extent of the danger she was in.

'Are you saying you don't want me any more?' she questioned shakily and heard his faint sigh in response.

'I'm saying no such thing, Ellie. I don't want to lose you. Of course I want you. I would never have asked you to move in if I didn't. But only you. Just because I want to share my home and my life with you doesn't mean that I'm prepared to consider starting a family and becoming a father.'

At the time it had been enough. That 'only you', spoken

in that deep, dark, huskily intent tone had lifted her spirits, setting her heart singing. Morgan had actually said that he wanted her to share his home—*and his life*! That he didn't want to lose her. She would be all kinds of a fool to think of asking for anything more.

'And I would never want it to be other than just the two of us.'

She even managed a smile, slid a hint of throatily seductive invitation into her voice.

'I could never share you with anyone else.'

To her intense relief, the tight line of his mouth relaxed slightly. The darkness that had shaded his eyes eased gradually, changing his expression subtly.

'Couldn't you?'

'Oh, no...'

She felt on firmer ground now, her confidence growing as one warm, strong hand slid under the golden fall of her hair to curl around her neck, drawing her closer, gently but irresistibly.

The touch of his lips on her forehead made her heart skip a beat and she tilted her head so that her cheek rested against the heat of his palm. Looking up at him through the fringe of her eyelashes, she slanted a glance that was pure feminine enticement into the luminous blue of his eyes.

'I want you all to myself.'

'In that case...' Morgan's response was a harshly sensual growl as his grip tightened in her hair, holding her a willing prisoner '...I think we're both getting exactly what we want out of this relationship.'

And from that moment all conversation was abandoned as his mouth came down hard on hers.

There was an exciting difference about his kiss this time, the fierce demand that always sent the heavy, honeyed pulse of desire throbbing through her veins mixed with a new and unexpected tenderness that raced straight to Ellie's vulnerable heart like an arrow thudding into the gold centre on a target.

Perhaps it was that she was so sharply aware of how close a call she had had, how near she had come to losing this relationship, that made her feel things so much more. Or perhaps that fear had given a new edge to her emotions, leaving her in no doubt that Morgan was as essential to her well-being as the air she breathed.

Either way, the passion that flared between them as Morgan crushed her mouth under his was white-hot and all consuming, searing through every nerve in her body, setting her blood aflame with sensation so powerfully and so fast that she feared her bones might actually melt in the fiercely incandescent conflagration.

With her head spinning, her body clamouring hungrily for more of the glorious delights it was experiencing, she was scarcely aware of Morgan swinging her up into his arms and carrying her upstairs.

'This is what I want—what we both want...' he muttered as he laid her on the bed, stripping her clothes from her with urgently efficient hands, pressing swift, demanding kisses on the pale flesh he exposed, licking, sucking, nipping. 'This is what makes what we have special—what will keep us together.'

The passion that raged through Ellie like fire through a tinder-dry forest drove all thought of hesitancy or restraint before it, giving her a new sense of confidence, a desire to show the true depths of her feelings. That need directed her instinctively, giving her new ways to touch, to caress, to kiss him, arousing him to the point where he so completely forgot himself that he cried her name out loud in the moment of fulfilment. In the same split second Ellie felt as if her whole being had been blasted into a myriad tiny pieces, scattered to every corner of the universe as she tumbled crazily into the deepest, darkest abyss of sensation.

It was a long, long time before the violent cyclone of delight gradually slowed enough to allow her to have any awareness of the real world once again. And when she did come back down to earth, she felt as if something cataclysmic and totally life-changing had happened.

It was as if all those myriads of tiny pieces of herself had come together to form a new being that, while it was externally the same as the Ellie she had been earlier that night, could never, ever be exactly the same as it had been before.

'Ma! Ma-ma-ma-ma-ma!'

Beside her, Rosie's loud babbling and a renewed drumming of red-shoed heels against the base of the pushchair brought her back out of the past and reminded her that in the present her daughter was getting impatient.

'I'm sorry, sweetie!' she said penitently. 'I know—I promised we would go out just as soon as I've finished this. One more minute and Mummy will be ready.'

She had raised the topic of children again, she recalled as she hurried to hang the rest of the washing on the line, but not for a long time. The fright she'd had had meant that in the future she'd been wary of risking opening any subject that might have driven a wedge between them, destroying the happiness she'd so delighted in. And when she had risked questioning Morgan again it had been only too clear that his attitude hadn't changed.

Not that he'd ever actually *discussed* it with her. Sometimes he'd simply blocked the idea, refusing even to be drawn into talking about anything by declaring that he'd had work to do or a phone call to make. More often than not, he would use the same sort of diversionary tactics he had employed the first time, subjecting her to the sort of sensual onslaught that had set a sexual hunger raging through her and left her incapable of any form of thought for a very long time.

No!

Shaking her head roughly to clear her thoughts, Ellie refused to let herself dwell on the past any more. What she
needed was a distraction.

'Come on, darling,' she said, turning the pushchair in the
direction of the front door. 'Let's go and ring Vicki and see
if she'll meet us in Truro. It'll do us good to get out and
about for a while.'

She'd made the right decision all those months ago, she
told herself as she cleaned and changed her daughter ready
for their trip out. It was impossible to bear the thought that
Rosie might never have been born, and that was what she
had most feared might happen if she had told Morgan about
her pregnancy. Even to think of the 'solution' he might have
put forward made her stomach heave with bitter nausea, and
she had known that she would *hate* Morgan for ever if he
had so much as suggested the idea of an abortion.

It had been bad enough as it was.

Her hands stilled on the wriggling little body, all colour
leaching from her face as she recalled the moment that
Morgan had very nearly caught her out.

Knowing that her period had already been overdue and
suspecting the worst, Ellie had secretly bought a pregnancy-
testing kit from the chemist during her lunch break. But on
the journey home from work that evening she had suddenly
been assailed by an attack of sickness that had had her dropping her bag on the kitchen table, heedless of the way it
fell on its side, scattering its contents onto the floor and
dashing upstairs to the bathroom.

It had been fully ten minutes before she'd been fit to go
back downstairs again and by that time Morgan had come
home. Ellie had arrived in the doorway just in time to see
him bend to pick up the selection of items that had fallen
from her bag. Her heart had leapt into her throat, the blood
pounding in her head, as he'd straightened up again, the
testing kit in his hand.

'What is this?' he asked, and just the sound of his voice turned her blood to ice as a cold, cruel hand twisted her heart inside her chest. 'Are you pregnant?'

'No!'

What other answer could she give? If she had any doubts at all that his determination was still fixed, any hope of a softening in his resolution, they fled in the moment she looked into his face. His expression said it all.

Horrified shock, dark anger and total rejection of the possibility of her pregnancy were stamped into every line, etched on the forceful bone structure, pulling his skin tight across his cheekbones. If anything, it seemed that his conviction had hardened over the intervening months, and only the world's greatest fool would put any faith in the possibility of his welcoming the news of her condition.

'Me, pregnant? No way!'

She didn't know how she managed it but somehow she actually injected a note of laughter into her response.

'Don't be daft, Morgan! How could I be pregnant? I've been on the pill for over nine months.'

Nine months apart from two days, a small, malicious voice whispered in her ear, reminding her of the time, just over six weeks before, when she had been flattened by a rare, blinding migraine and for the first time ever had forgotten to take the pill she otherwise remembered so scrupulously.

'And the last thing I'd want is to have a baby right now,' she bluffed desperately. 'Janet's seriously thinking of offering me the partnership in the agency—and you know how much I've wanted that.'

This was better. That last declaration had at least sounded more convincing—mainly because it was the truth and Morgan knew it. She *had* dreamed of going into partnership with Janet, the owner of the agency, and had been putting in a lot of overtime in the hope that the prospect might actually be on the cards.

'Then what is this doing here?'

'This?'

Ellie went through a performance of taking the package from him, opening it, and looking inside as if she actually didn't remember what it contained. She thought about affecting a small start of surprise but in the end decided that that would be just too much.

'Oh, that...'

Casually she tossed it back into the open neck of her bag, dragging up a dismissive laugh and forcing herself to turn away and pick up the kettle, heading for the sink to fill it.

'That's Tracy's. She's six days late and panicking like mad. She bought that at lunchtime when we were out together and I let her put it in my bag so she didn't have to carry it into the office. I must have forgotten to give it back to her. I'll give her a ring later to let her know I have it. Coffee?'

For a worrying, nerve-stretching count of six he didn't answer and she knew that her response was being considered, weighed up inside that cool, incisive brain while he decided whether to believe her or not.

'Okay,' he said at last. 'Coffee would be good.' And the fierce rush of relief at hearing the tension in his voice ease was like a blow to her head, making it spin wildly for a second or two.

She'd had to force that coffee down, Ellie remembered now. The changes in her body as a result of her pregnancy had meant that she had come to detest both the smell and the taste of what had once been her favourite drink.

That day had been the beginning of the end. Ellie's eyes blurred with unshed tears at the pain of the memory. She had struggled on for another couple of weeks, trying desperately not to let her feelings show. She had had to resort to endless tricks and subterfuges to hide the sickness that had plagued her every day, use more make-up than usual to disguise the ashen pallor of her cheeks.

It had only been when, while getting dressed one morning, she'd noted that the waistband on her skirt had been just that little bit tight, that she'd realised she couldn't pretend any more. She couldn't take the risk that Morgan would notice the changes in her and start to question them.

But she hadn't been able to stop herself from making one last, desperate attempt to talk to Morgan. Stumblingly, hesitantly, she had broached the subject of their future, using the prospect of the partnership in the agency as an excuse.

'I need to know if there are likely to be any—changes—in the future that might affect my decision...'

There was no need for him to answer. Her heart seemed to die inside her as she looked into the chilling ice-blue of his eyes and knew with a terrible despair that his mind was as set as before.

'If you're trying to ask if I feel any differently about having children, then the answer is no. Nothing has changed. It's just you and me, angel, and that's the way I like it.'

And Ellie forced a smile and said that that was how she liked it too.

That was when she turned to her friend Pete for help. And Pete's advice was succinct and to the point.

'You're going to have to leave him, Ellie,' he said sombrely. 'You know you have no alternative. You've already given your heart to this baby. It would kill you if you had to give it up.'

Yes, Ellie told herself now, she'd given Rosie all her heart and from the moment of the baby's birth she had been caught up in such a maelstrom of love that she just couldn't bear even to imagine life without this small person in it.

But giving her heart to Rosie didn't mean erasing the love

that had been in it for Morgan. A love she had felt, still felt, and would always feel. But she could never admit to that love. To do so would be to risk blowing open the secret she had kept at such a personal cost for so long.

CHAPTER SIX

MORGAN saw the car arrive just as he was about to lose patience.

He had been sitting in the car outside the farmhouse for over twenty minutes now and was frankly bored. Nothing but a fierce determination to see Ellie again and have things out with her would have kept him there for that length of time, but it had looked as if, wherever she had gone, she planned to stay for the rest of the afternoon.

He was just leaning forward to insert his key into the ignition when he heard the muted roar of another engine and stilled, waiting.

She'd obviously been out with a friend. The driver of the battered Land Rover was another woman, long, bright auburn hair tumbling down over her shoulders. Ellie was laughing as she pushed opened the passenger door and got out, the sound carrying easily on the bright summer air.

It twisted something deep in Morgan's guts at the thought of how long it was since he had heard that particular sound. How long it was since he had heard Ellie laugh with that light-hearted freedom of feeling. And not just because the two of them had been apart for so long. There had been no laughter in the home they had shared for weeks before she had finally picked up the courage to tell him she was leaving. Instead her mood had been so very difficult, withdrawn and unapproachable.

Crushing down the memories he didn't want to recall, Morgan pushed open his own car door with a violence that would have shocked the friends who knew the care he usually took of the sleek, powerful vehicle.

'I'll take the shopping inside…'

Ellie's voice, still with that disturbing bubble of laughter running through it, drifted clearly over the grass towards him.

'Have you got time for a coffee before you get back? Yes? Well, why don't you bring Rosie in, then, and I'll put the kettle on?'

Morgan scowled faintly, hesitating just for a moment. What he wanted was Ellie all to himself. What he had to say wasn't suitable for an audience, and certainly not a female friend who might be inclined to chatter and spread gossip.

But it was too late to turn back now. Any minute Ellie or her friend might spot him and, damn it, he didn't want to wait. The last few days had been a very particular form of hell, one he had no desire to go back into. He hadn't been able to work or think straight. He hadn't even been able to sleep properly. It had been like taking several long, uncomfortable steps back into the past, finding himself once again in the sort of frustrated empty limbo that had plagued him just after Ellie had left the first time.

Perhaps talking to Ellie with her friend there might have unexpected bonuses. The other girl might just let slip something that Ellie herself had kept hidden; something she didn't want him to know.

Because she was hiding things from him, he didn't doubt that for a moment. She had deliberately misled him about Pete for one thing, and he wouldn't rest until he found out precisely why.

'Come on, then, Rosie, sweetheart…'

The redhead was leaning into the back seat of the car, unaware of his approach. Morgan gave a small, warning cough.

'Hi,' he said quietly.

She whirled round, blue eyes widening in slight shock, but she adjusted quickly enough.

'Hi yourself,' she returned with a smiling glance up through her eyelashes.

He knew that look. He ought to do. He'd encountered it often enough on publicity tours or more recently in the film or television studios where he'd met what seemed like an endless stream of young, ambitious women, all of whom had been flatteringly pleased to see him.

He knew why, of course. The attractions of sudden, dramatic success, the sort of success that had brought with it an income it would take several lifetimes to get through, were only too obvious. The fact that he was the right side of fifty and didn't exactly look like the back of a bus helped too. And because he was known to be single, with no girlfriend or live-in lover in sight, he was regarded, as one girl had said, 'as an intriguing challenge'.

Many women, some stunningly attractive, some less so, had tried to rise to that challenge, and for a time he'd let some of them into his life. But nothing had lasted. They had never been more than ships that had passed in the night, pleasant enough to spend time with for a while, to hold back the emptiness that had swirled in his mind if he'd let his guard down for a moment. But they had never driven away that emptiness for good.

Only one woman had ever done that. Only one woman had seemed to offer him a hope of a future, and, just when he had begun to believe that that future might have had a hope of being permanent, she had snatched it right away from him.

But the redhead he knew how to handle.

'I'm Morgan Stafford,' he said, directing his smile straight into those big blue eyes.

'I guessed you were our visiting celebrity. I've been hearing all about you. I'm Vicki, by the way—Vicki Jefferson...'

Coming back down the hallway from the kitchen where she had dumped the bags of shopping, Ellie caught the sound of Morgan's voice, recognising it instantly, and stopped dead in shock, her heart kicking painfully.

Through the open door she could see his tall, lean frame, the long legs encased in well-worn denim jeans, a spotless white tee shirt tucked into the leather belt that encircled the narrow waist. A faint breeze had tossed his glossy dark hair, lifting it and blowing it forward onto the high, broad forehead.

Morgan! And *Rosie*—oh, dear God, Rosie was still in the car. Still fastened securely in her own safety seat, her hands waving wildly, impatient feet kicking in protest at being restrained.

Rosie...

She didn't know what she was going to say. How she was going to react. She couldn't move, couldn't think, the only coherent sound that formed inside her head that of her daughter's name as if somehow she could warn the baby just who was near.

But she couldn't utter it. Her tongue had frozen, her vocal cords shrivelled in sheer blind panic.

Months before, on the day of Rosie's birth, she had taken her baby in her arms for the very first time and wept aching, yearning bitter tears to think that her beautiful little girl would never set eyes on the man who was her father. But now Morgan was here, the moment she had dreamed about had actually come to be, and she was shivering from sheer terror just at the thought of it.

And as she stood, struggling even to make her gaze focus on the scene in front of her, Rosie let out one wild, sharply impatient shriek that brought Vicki's bright head swinging round.

'Oh, sorry, sweetie—was I ignoring you? Are you sick and tired of that nasty seat?'

Vicki—no...

But the protest evaporated into a silent, formless croak and she still couldn't force her frozen muscles into action.

'Who's Rosie?'

She heard Morgan's question as if from the far end of a long, long tunnel. It sounded disjointed and blurred by the roaring inside her head.

She wanted to dash out there and snatch up her daughter into her arms. Wanted to turn and run, take the baby far, far from here. Wanted to fold her arms protectively around the small, sturdy body and protect Rosie from all harm, any harm, even the unknowing slight of letting Morgan's cold, indifferent gaze fall on her delicate baby skin.

But in the same second she also wanted to go out there and lift the baby from her safety seat. To turn and face the tall, dark man defiantly. To look him straight in the eye and declare, 'This is Rosie, Morgan. This is your daughter.'

But all her strength had deserted her; her will failed her. She could only watch as Vicki reached into the back seat of the Land Rover and emerged clutching a small, wriggling body.

'This little charmer is Rosie.'

Charmer was the word, Morgan reflected silently as he found himself being studied for the second time by a pair of wide, intrigued blue eyes. This Vicki's kid was seriously cute. But it was more than that. There was something in that wide-eyed, almost comically solemn stare that caught unexpectedly on some raw part of his feelings.

Rosie was pure female, a tiny, barely formed beauty that tugged at something deep inside, some primitive, totally instinctive masculine need to defend and protect. Those amazing eyes were fringed by the thickest, darkest lashes, almost ridiculously luxuriant on someone so small, and the baby's hair was as dark and glossy as polished ebony. The tiny rosebud mouth was the softest pink, the delicate skin peach-smooth.

Ellie's skin had had the same downy softness. Her eyes had had the same brilliant glow, though of course hers had burned like polished amber, not this clear, luminous sapphire...

A feeling like a sudden blow to his chest drove all the air from his body in a gasping breath. Under other circumstances, at another time, another place, this baby could have been Ellie's and...

No!

Automatically he pulled himself up short, slamming the door shut on the thoughts that had almost escaped his normally rigid control. He didn't think about such things. He'd never let himself even consider them—except once.

What the hell was happening to him?

No, he knew the answer to that. It had been like this ever since Ellie had come into his life. Before Ellie, he had never had to think, just react, switching off unwanted feelings with the ease of long practice, but since she had left he had found it difficult to go back to the way he had once lived.

'Hi, Rosie,' he managed with a carelessness that he hoped was convincing.

A sudden faint sound, a hint of movement to his left, caught his eye and had him turning swiftly, darkened blue eyes meeting Ellie's cool golden stare in a moment of intense awareness that pounded another mental punch into the pit of his stomach.

'Your tenant's come to see you,' Vicki put in cheerfully, blithely oblivious to the sudden singing tension, the tightening of the atmosphere until it seemed that the air was almost impossible to breathe.

'So I see.' Ellie had no idea how she forced the words

out. 'What can I do for you, Mr Stafford? Have you come for milk—or eggs?'

How *could* she speak about something so matter of fact, so banal, when her mind was in such turmoil?

What she really needed to know was what Morgan was thinking. What was he *feeling*? Was it possible that he could have looked at Rosie and not seen himself reflected in the baby's face, the perfect, tiny feminised replica of his features that she saw so clearly every day?

'No, nothing like that.'

She looked like he felt—damn awful. As if, like him, she hadn't had a decent night's sleep since their encounter at the cottage. But not for the same reasons, of course. It was highly unlikely that she had been a prey to the erotic dreams, the heated, sensual images, the savage hunger that had clawed at him in the darkness of the night. The desire that was always there, just below the surface, that even now, just to see her, was stinging in his blood, tightening his body in hard, swift response to her nearness.

'I wanted to talk to you about that housekeeper you insisted I employed instead of you. The one you said would suit me perfectly.'

'Is there a problem?'

It was a struggle to get her thoughts to focus. Had the moment she had alternately dreamed of with a desperate hope and dreaded with a sense of darkly oppressive fear actually come and gone with all the effect of a damp squib? Had Morgan, for the first time ever, set eyes on his child, his own flesh and blood, and not even turned a hair?

But then, what had she expected? Had she really believed that he would take one look at Rosie and fall in love with her in the blink of an eye? That he would have immediately gathered her into his arms with a cry of recognition, tears of remorse for the time they had lost burning in his eyes?

She had to have been deceiving herself foolishly if she'd even dreamed that it might happen.

'You're damn right there's a problem. She doesn't suit me at all. She is incapable of leaving a single piece of paper where she finds it. She insists on "tidying" everything into neat, regimented piles, with the result that I can't find a damn thing I want.'

'I'm sorry... Vicki, why don't you take Rosie inside? The kettle should have boiled by now if you want to make the coffee... So what, precisely, do you want me to do about the situation?' she demanded of Morgan as her friend and the baby disappeared inside.

'I told you what I wanted from the beginning. I never wanted this Dee or anyone else to act as housekeeper for me.'

'And I told you I wouldn't do the job! Perhaps Nan...'

'No way.' Morgan shook his arrogant dark head in total rejection of whatever suggestion she had been about to make. 'I told you, Ellie—'

'*You* told me!' Ellie's precarious grip on her volatile temper snapped completely. 'I know only too well what you told me—what *you* want. But unfortunately, Morgan, we can't always have exactly what we want. I do have other responsibilities besides fulfilling your excessive demands, and nurturing your ego!'

'Nurturing!' His response was a snort of laughter. 'Lady, you were the one who kicked my ego right into touch, stamping on it and crushing it into tiny little pieces.'

'Well, I'm sure it recovered pretty quickly...'

With her attention more than half on the sounds from the kitchen where the small, boisterous reason for her 'kicking his ego into touch' was loudly making her presence felt, Ellie was finding it hard to concentrate.

'Now if that's all...'

'As a matter of fact it's not.'

'Then what…?'

Something about his tone caught on her nerves and when she looked into his face her heart jolted uncomfortably.

'You didn't really come here to talk about Dee, did you?'

'It wasn't at the top of my list, no,' Morgan returned with a sardonic grin. 'For one thing I wanted to return these…'

Ellie could only stare in horror at the small bundle he pulled from his pocket. Folded neatly into the palm of his hand, white satin and lace in stark contrast to the tanned skin of his fingers, was something she recognised immediately. A hot wash of colour spread through her cheeks as she remembered how in her headlong flight from the cottage she had left her panties and bra discarded somewhere on Morgan's bedroom floor.

'Coffee's ready!' Vicki's shout broke into the long moment of silence. 'Come on, you two.'

Two? 'Oh, but…' She had had no intention of inviting Morgan in for coffee as well.

Her protest died unformed as, ignoring her obvious disapproval, Morgan headed off down the hall. It took her a couple of seconds to realise that he still carried her underwear crushed in his hand. Hastily she forced herself into movement, running to catch up with him, and snatching them away as quickly as she could.

'I'll take those!'

It made her blood run cold just to think of what Vicki would make of his appearing in the kitchen, still in possession of her underwear.

'One coffee, that's all.'

In all the time that she had known Vicki Jefferson, Ellie would have said that she had never once envied her friend her long auburn hair and vivid blue eyes. But now, seeing Morgan with his eyes fixed on the other girl's face, his smile warm with open appreciation, she knew with a sickening jolt that the sensation clawing at her was nothing more than bitter jealousy. Jealousy that burned like acid.

Once, he had looked at her like that, smiled that smile for her. Once he had concentrated his attention on her in just that way, made her feel as if the rest of the world had faded away, as if they'd been the only two people in existence.

'I gave guzzleguts a drink, and one of her biscuits, if that's okay.'

Vicki dragged her attention away from Morgan with obvious reluctance to nod towards Rosie who was sitting in her high chair, sucking contentedly on a bottle of juice.

'Oh, and before I forget, Mum said could I take back a dozen eggs for her?'

'No problem.' Ellie picked up a basket from the worktop. 'You know where to find them—help yourself.'

It was like being on an emotional see-saw, she reflected ruefully. One moment she had been plagued by jealousy, wishing Vicki anywhere but here. Now, with her friend gone from the room to collect the eggs, she felt painfully vulnerable and alone, supremely conscious of Morgan's silent, watchful presence in his seat at the kitchen table. Her skin seemed to prickle at the back of her neck, almost as if his gaze had a physical touch, scouring over her skin.

And to make matters worse she still had her underwear in her jeans pocket, carefully hidden from Vicki's interested eyes.

Angrily pushing it further in, wishing she could push away her memories with the same ease, she turned her attention to Rosie, moving to unfasten the light cotton jacket the baby wore and ease it from the small body.

'There, that's better, isn't it?' she said to the little girl who beamed back brightly revealing the few teeth she possessed. 'You were too warm with that on in here.'

'How old is she?'

Morgan's question caught her unawares, throwing her thoughts into instant panic. Not like this, she thought desperately. Not here, not now—not yet!

'She's eight months.'

Oh, what had she done? There was no going back now, and she could only pray that, like most men, Morgan wasn't well up in child development and so wouldn't guess at the three months she had lopped off her daughter's existence.

'Eight and a half,' she added hastily, needing to make a small concession to the truth. 'She's quite big—and advanced for her age.'

It seemed that with every word she spoke she dug herself deeper and deeper into a pit from which she was going to find it impossible to escape. From the moment she had spoken the first lie she had known she was going to have to weave a web of them, and if she wasn't careful they were going to tangle round her, threatening to choke her.

'Gah!'

Rosie made her contribution to the conversation by shrieking at the top of her voice and flinging her rattle straight at Morgan. The brightly-coloured toy bounced on his shoulder and only his fast reflexes meant that he caught it before it landed on the floor.

Now what? Ellie could hardly bear to watch, every nerve stretched tight, as he turned and held it out to Rosie again. Two pairs of sapphire eyes locked for an endless couple of seconds, the baby's holding a mixture of curiosity and suspicion, Morgan's impossible to read, before a plump hand reached out and snatched the rattle back.

'Gah!' she said, as if offering some form of thanks before pushing the handle into her mouth and sucking on it enthusiastically.

'And gah to you,' Morgan returned with a totally unexpected lightness.

Ellie's vision blurred suddenly and she had to turn away,

pretending to be looking for a sugar spoon so as to hide the hot, betraying tears that stung her eyes. It was the smile that had done the damage. It wasn't much of a smile, just a tiny flicker of amusement at the corners of Morgan's sensual mouth, but it had shattered her composure, making her want to moan aloud in distress.

Would that smile still be there if he knew the truth? Or would the knowledge that he was Rosie's father wipe all warmth from his mind once and for all?

'She's a pretty little thing,' Morgan said from behind her, his matter-of-fact tone revealing his total lack of awareness of the anguished turmoil she was struggling with. 'I assume that she takes after her father?'

'I—she…'

Oh, God, just how did she answer that? All that she could manage was a faint, wordless croak that he would have to interpret any way he wanted.

'After all, she's not very like her mother. Her hair's almost black, not a trace of Vicki's red…'

The rest of his words faded into an unintelligible blur as the truth hit home like a blow to the head.

Morgan believed that Rosie was *Vicki's* daughter! He never even suspected that Ellie had anything to do with her, let alone that she might possibly be his own flesh and blood. And the lie about Rosie's age that she had told in a moment of panic would only seem to confirm that belief.

The pit she had dug for herself was growing deeper by the second.

CHAPTER SEVEN

ELLIE couldn't force her thoughts to focus on anything other than the immediate, very practical matters in hand.

'Sugar...' she muttered, reminding herself what she was looking for, using the word like a primitive incantation against evil. 'Sugar, sugar, sugar.'

Forcing herself to turn round again, she dumped the sugar bowl on the table and sat down, refusing to meet Morgan's eyes. Still with her gaze averted, she poured coffee for herself and for him, automatically adding cream and one sugar to his mug and stirring it thoroughly before pushing it across the table.

It was only when his silence forced her to glance upwards and she saw the way he was looking at her that she realised what she'd done and coloured fiercely.

'Old habits die hard,' she managed shakily.

Old habits.

The description was like a slap in the face, making Morgan clench his hands in instinctive reaction out of sight beneath the protecting wood of the table. Talk about damning with faint praise! It seemed that with almost every word she spoke, Ellie added further fuel to his conviction that he had made the right decision to hold back, to keep his most private thoughts from her, even in the time they'd been together.

'Is that all I was?' he asked softly. 'A habit?'

In which case, what the hell was he doing here, letting his ego be taken out and trampled on all over again? What sort of a fool was he? Was he going to lie down and let her walk all over him once more?

'Oh—no... You were right... At the beginning we had something...something special...'

'Only at the beginning?'

Morgan's dark head moved, came closer, his brilliant gaze holding hers transfixed, lacking the strength even to blink.

'So what went wrong?'

'Morgan. Please don't...' she whispered, her voice just a thin thread of sound. But he caught it and leaned even further across the table, his powerful forearms resting on the light wood, his hands so close to hers that she could almost feel the heat of his skin burning into her.

His physical nearness was affecting her terribly, making her heart pound, disturbing her breathing so that he had to be aware of the difficulty she was having to bring herself under control.

'Don't what, angel? Don't ask awkward questions? But what if I want to know the answers? Don't you think I have the right to know the truth?'

'The...'

Ellie turned wide, shocked bronze eyes on his closed, unyielding face, unable to believe that she had heard right.

'The truth,' Morgan repeated implacably. 'The real reason why that ''something special'' died.'

'But I did! I told—'

At his violently muttered curse, she broke off in shock.

'I told you...' she whispered in desperation. 'About Pete...'

'No.'

Morgan shook his dark head in violent negation.

'You told me nothing about Pete. *I* told you.'

'You...'

Ellie slumped into a chair, her legs going from beneath her, a buzzing like a thousand angry bees whirling inside her head.

'I was the one who brought Pete into it when you said you were leaving,' Morgan told her, willing her to listen, really listen, and not just to fly into one of the angry protestations that he was now sure were just smokescreens, used to hide her real feelings.

And they had worked. Earlier, at the cottage, and even more so on the day that she had announced she was leaving, he had let her anger, the vehemence with which she had spoken, blind him to the fact that her heart hadn't been fully in what she'd been saying. Or if not her heart, then at least all of her mind.

But later, in the cool, lonely isolation of the night, when he had had too much time to think, he had reviewed the scenes between them, replaying them over and over on a loop inside his head. And this time he had seen things. Things that he hadn't noticed the first time round. Things that he had been too proud, too damn proud to see.

'*I* was the first to mention Pete. *I* put the words in your mouth because I couldn't believe that you could just fall out of love with me—that your feelings could shrivel and die like that. *I* asked if there was someone else and if that someone else was Pete. You'd always been so close to him, and in those last few months you were always with him. It seemed that you could talk to him when you couldn't talk to me.'

'Morgan...'

Despairingly Ellie closed her eyes against the fierce scrutiny of that blazing gaze, wishing she could shut out the misery of her memories as easily.

If she only had herself to think of, then she would have welcomed this so much. How many times over the past eighteen months had she let herself fantasise that perhaps, one day, Morgan would come to her and say that he had got things wrong? That he had accused her of being unfaithful, of cheating on him with Pete, only out of pain, because he had misinterpreted things so badly.

In her dreams she had been able to explain. She had been able to tell him the truth, explain all his misapprehensions and they had been able to start again.

But that was where the dream parted company with reality. Because Rosie was part of the equation now and as a result it would never, ever balance out again.

'But I should have known that Pete wasn't what you wanted—that he couldn't give you enough.'

'Give!'

Ellie's head came up sharply, her eyes hot at the implications behind his words.

'Give me what?'

But Morgan was already rushing on, blatantly ignoring her interjection, sweeping it aside with an arrogant wave of his hand.

'If he could, you wouldn't be here, working on this farm, obviously with no money to buy yourself clothes...'

Did he really believe this? Could he truly not see that it had not been his *wealth* that had drawn her to him? Anger was a violent blaze in Ellie's mind, driving away the conciliatory thoughts, the dreams of just moments before.

'And just why should my reasons for leaving you matter any more? After all, to you I was just... What was it?'

Her hesitation was pure pretence. She had no need to struggle to remember the words; they were branded into her thoughts in letters of fire.

'The biggest mistake you ever made in your life! So why should it worry you *why* I wanted out too?'

Except perhaps that she had stung his male pride by being the one who had walked out on the great Morgan Stafford. Women just didn't do that to him. He made all the running, did the seducing, the loving, the leaving.

'I couldn't bear to live with you any longer!' she flung

at him. 'We didn't share the same values any more; we didn't want the same things from life. I was living a lie and I couldn't lie any more!'

A terrible, brittle silence followed her outburst, one that stretched every nerve to breaking-point, and yet she couldn't think of a single way to break it. She didn't even dare to look at Morgan, terrified of the black fury she knew must show in his face.

And she couldn't look at Rosie sitting beside her, happily making a soggy mess of her biscuit and smearing it all over her face. To her mind, the baby had never looked more like some tiny, feminised mirror image of her father, threatening the few ragged remnants of the self-control she was struggling to clutch to her.

'Morgan—say something.'

'Say something,' he echoed, his voice low and loaded with dark savagery. 'Say something? I reckon you've said everything there is to say on the matter.'

Every damn thing there was to say. Just for a second there, he'd thought they might be getting somewhere. That they might actually be beginning to talk.

Oh, she'd talked all right! 'I couldn't bear to live with you any longer.' Well, he damn well wasn't going to put his head on the block a second time.

'I…' Ellie began, but whatever she had been about to say was broken off as Rosie, bored with sitting in her chair, and confused by the angry undertones in which the conversation had been carried out, took matters into her own small hands.

'Bah!' she shrieked, turning her bright blue eyes towards Morgan once more.

This time it was a well-sucked portion of biscuit that she threw with deadly accuracy straight onto the immaculate whiteness of his tee shirt.

'Rosie!' Ellie remonstrated in horror. 'Oh, I'm sorry.'

Where had this sudden wild streak in her usually well-behaved daughter come from? It was almost as if Rosie sensed the atmosphere, knew that this was a time when she should be at her most delightful, her winning best, and had set herself to be the opposite.

In that, at least, she was very like her father, Ellie reflected ruefully, as, snatching up a tea towel, she tried to wipe away the sticky mess.

And immediately knew it was a mistake as all her senses went into overdrive. The scent of Morgan's body enveloped her, and she was so close that she could hear the steady beat of his heart under the white material. Even through the medium of the cotton pad, she was intensely aware of the width of bone, the hard power of muscle. The tension she could sense in the strong body was infinitely disturbing, and the sudden freezing of Morgan's breathing sharply mirrored her own response.

'It'll wash,' she said nervously, struggling with a feeling like the build-up of pressure inside a volcano, only seconds away from erupting.

'Do you think I give a damn?' Morgan's voice was curiously constrained. 'It's only a tee shirt…'

Surely she knew that it wasn't the damage to his clothing that bothered him in the least. Didn't she realise what it did to him to have her bent over him like this, her golden head so close to his face that he could inhale the soft scent of her hair? Surely she must sense the struggle he was having to control his body's instinctive responses, the way the muscles in his jaw tightened, his hands clenching against the urge to grab her, haul her up against him and kiss her stupid.

Over Ellie's downbent head his eyes met the bright, inquisitive ones of the baby in the high chair. She was watching him, head on one side, like an alert, intrigued little bird.

Come on, kid! he telegraphed with his eyes. *Get me out of this!*

'Bah! Gah!'

Rosie let fly with another soggy missile, making Ellie start up, and Morgan dodge back. Ellie closed her eyes in despair as she saw the sticky mess land in the shining ebony strands of his hair and slide down onto his face. But a moment later she opened them wide again, blinking in disbelief because the sound Morgan had made had sounded suspiciously like a suppressed chuckle.

When she risked a glance at his face, she was stunned to see that he was struggling to hold back laughter, his eyes gleaming with genuine amusement.

'She has a wonderful line in conversation,' he said, his voice shaking as he fought for control. This sort of control, though, was much easier to manage, and at least it distracted him from other, less comfortable feelings. 'Though I can't help wondering just what I've done to earn the honour of being used for target practice in this way. Is she like this with everyone, or is it just me?'

'She's showing off.' Ellie's voice came and went like a faulty radio as she struggled with this unexpected development. 'I—think it means she likes you.'

'Then I wish she'd find some other way of expressing her feelings. Rosie—no!'

His voice changed suddenly, and, swivelling round, Ellie saw the plastic bottle, still half full of orange juice, being lifted, aimed...

'Rosie!'

Together she and Morgan lunged, his greater speed and longer arms enabling him to capture the missile before it was launched. With an exaggerated sigh of relief he dropped back into his chair, setting the bottle down on the table.

Over the baby's head their eyes met in a moment of such warmth and shared understanding that Ellie's heart clenched sharply, twisting in her chest. Her mind felt hazy, spinning with the thought that the whole world had been rocked dangerously, turned upside down and inside out so that she no longer knew which was up and what was down and had no idea whether she was on her head or her heels.

Time froze; even her heart seemed to stand still, her breathing faint and shallow, and endless questions beat against her brain, none of them offering any sort of an answer.

Was it possible that she had been wrong to despair? That she need never have left Morgan in the first place? Could it be that, although Morgan might reject the idea of children in theory, the reality of his daughter, who had so far charmed everyone she met, might prove so much harder to resist?

'I think peace has been declared.' Morgan's tone was wry as he rubbed the last pieces of biscuit from his hair. 'Either that or she's just run out of weapons.'

Her mind still too full to think, Ellie could only manage a wordless murmur, her stomach tying itself in knots as she saw the way that, hearing him speak, Rosie turned towards Morgan and treated him to her most endearing, gummy grin. That smile melted anyone within ten paces—but would it have the desired effect on Morgan?

And what, a tiny unwanted voice questioned at the back of her mind, what will you do if Morgan comes to accept his child but not her mother? How will you cope then?

She'd cope! she told herself, pushing the thought away. She'd have to!

But all her resolve evaporated, her heart clenching agonisingly, as she watched Morgan lean towards the baby.

'You, madam,' he said with mock severity, 'are a rogue and a villain.'

Totally unabashed, Rosie beamed again, then, leaning forward, extended a sticky hand and patted her father gently on the cheek.

Ellie could take no more. Digging her teeth into her bottom lip to bite back the moan of distress that almost escaped her, she whirled away, blinded by burning tears that she was desperate to hide.

Somehow her thoughts worked enough to remind her that she needed a reason for her action, and, finding her coffee-cup close at hand, she grabbed hold of it and unceremoniously upended its contents into the sink.

'It had gone cold,' she muttered gruffly, rushing to forestall the inevitable question. 'Undrinkable...'

'Did you think I'd got lost?'

Never in her life had she been so profoundly grateful to see Vicki reappear, Ellie thought thankfully as her friend strolled into the kitchen again, carefully carrying a full basket of eggs.

'Your chickens have been going mad, Ellie, they'd laid dozens and dozens of eggs, so I thought I'd collect them all for you. That's why I've been so long. You should try these, Morgan,' she chattered on, oblivious to or simply ignoring the uncomfortable atmosphere that had greeted her arrival. 'The best eggs in the world—fresh from the nest.'

'I'll find a box to put yours in.'

Grateful for something to do, Ellie crossed to the large walk-in pantry and made a production out of looking for an egg box and placing the eggs in it with unnecessary care. Behind her she heard Morgan and Vicki start up a conversation about food, the sort of casual, relaxed conversation that two people who had only just met could indulge in while getting to know each other.

The sort of conversation she and Morgan had never been able to have, she reflected sadly. They had always been too intense, too involved about everything. From the moment they had met, they had struck sparks off each other. Ellie's pulse-rate had lurched into overdrive just at the first sight of Morgan and, looking into his darkened eyes, seeing the flare of hot interest that burned there, she had known it had been the same for him too.

Once again she felt the cruel stab of jealousy that had tormented her earlier with the recognition of Morgan's obvious interest in her friend. Even Rosie...

'Oh, damn!'

Ellie's cry of shocked distress brought her friend's head swinging round.

'What's the matter, Ellie? Something wrong?'

Somehow Ellie dragged up enough self-control to manage a casual laugh, even if it sounded decidedly ragged round the edges.

'Dropped an egg,' she declared with what she hoped was an airy insouciance. 'Splattered it all over the floor. Now I'll have to wipe it up.'

She's not very like her mother. Her hair's almost black, not a trace of Vicki's red... Morgan's words came back to haunt her, tormenting her with the recollection of the thought behind them.

When she had been so delighted by the faint beginnings of warmth in Morgan's response to Rosie, she had forgotten one vital, important factor, and that was that Morgan had believed from the start that their baby was *Vicki's* daughter—and that changed everything.

He had been reacting to what he thought was a stranger's child, someone he was totally uninvolved with. Or perhaps someone he *wanted* to be involved with. Morgan was attracted to her friend, that much was obvious. So was making friends with Rosie part of a campaign to make the other girl like him?

'Haven't you finished in there yet, Ellie?' Vicki said, coming to the pantry door and looking in. 'I have to go now, sweetie, sorry.'

'But...'

Too late, Ellie realised that there was no way she could get Vicki to stay until Morgan left without arousing suspicion. There was no way of escape now, and all she could do was wait for the storm to break.

Planting an affectionate kiss on her friend's cheek, Vicki waved a reluctant goodbye to Morgan.

'It's been nice meeting you...'

On her way to the door she paused to ruffle Rosie's hair and drop a kiss on the button nose.

'Bye, poppet, see you soon.'

The significance of the gesture hit home to Morgan just as the door closed. Out of the corner of her eye Ellie could see how he first froze, then turned to look at Rosie and eventually, disturbingly, straight into her own face.

The silence seemed endless, unbearable, plucking on each sensitive nerve in Ellie's body and dragging it out agonisingly to near breaking-point. She could almost hear Morgan's mind working, sorting through facts, reviewing the evidence, realising where he had gone wrong, revising—coming at last to the right, appalling conclusion.

Don't say anything, she pleaded with him silently in her thoughts. Please, please don't say anything. Just get up and go, walk out and leave me, if not in peace, at least with what's left of my heart intact.

But her wish was not granted. Instead, Morgan pushed back his chair slowly, the legs making an ugly scraping sound on the tiled floor that brought her head swinging round to him.

It was his eyes that shocked her most. In stark contrast to the colour-leached pallor of his cheeks, they burned like savage ice-blue flames, seeming to sear the delicate flesh from her face so that she flinched back away from their almost physical force, lifting one shaking hand to ward off the violent power of his fury.

'Rosie...' he said at last, his voice harsh and raw. 'She's... Damn you to hell, Ellie—she's *yours*!'

CHAPTER EIGHT

AT AROUND two a.m., Morgan finally gave up on the idea of sleep.

He'd had too many nights like this in the past. Too many hours spent tossing and turning, twisting in bedclothes that were too much to bear in the dark warmth. Too many thoughts that he didn't want, too many memories that set his blood pulsing, tormenting his body with the heavy, restless ache of desire.

It had been like this when Ellie had first left him, and then he had vowed that he would never, ever let another woman put him through that hell again.

'Never, ever, huh?'

Tossing back the bedclothes, he pulled on a pair of jeans, barely bothering to check they were fastened before he padded downstairs in bare feet. After all, who was there to see and be offended? Only the owls and rabbits and maybe an occasional badger. There wasn't a soul for miles around. Grabbing a can of lager from the fridge, he took it out to the front of the cottage, leaning against a tree as he drank, his gaze fixed on the distant view of the sea, glimmering in the moonlight.

'Never again,' he repeated on a note of self-mockery. 'So how come you've let it happen again—and with the same woman, dammit?'

Except that this time it was worse. This time there was no easy escape; no comfortable way out. This time there was no need to go hunting in his mind for possible reasons, probable explanations. The facts were there, right in front

86

of him. If Ellie had slapped him in the face with them, she couldn't have made them any clearer.

'Why?'

It had been the only thing he'd been able to think of to say when, eighteen months before, Ellie had come to him and said that she wanted to end their relationship. That she was leaving. That in fact she had already packed and had a taxi coming to collect her and her stuff any minute.

'Why?'

If he was honest he couldn't say he hadn't seen it coming.

Correction, he couldn't have said he hadn't seen *something* coming. It had been obvious that something had been on her mind for some weeks. She'd been distant and abstracted, her thoughts obviously elsewhere. But he'd been deep in the latest book, burning the midnight oil in order to meet a deadline that had been looming up far too fast.

He didn't normally leave things so late. But this had been the first novel he'd written since Ellie had moved in. He'd known he should have begun it months earlier, but he'd been distracted by the sheer delight of having her there, of hearing her singing softly to herself as she'd cooked, scenting her perfume when he'd walked into a room or simply seeing her curled up on the settee on the opposite side of the fireplace.

And having her there in his bed every night.

Not just at night. The temptations of that lush, feminine body had been too much to resist—not that he'd put up much of a struggle. She'd only had to look at him, to press a soft kiss onto his cheek, to trail a delicate hand over his hair, and he would forget what he was doing and gather her up in his arms, carrying her off to the bed, or the settee or the fireside rug, whichever had been nearest.

'Dammit!'

Morgan's fist clenched on the lager can, crushing it brutally. He knew he'd been preoccupied that last couple of weeks, but he had also thought that what he and Ellie had had was so special that it could survive anything.

Even Ellie's friendship with Pete.

Friendship was all it was, she'd assured him.

'Pete's my brother Daniel's oldest friend. I've known him since my schooldays. I grew up with him! He's been teaching in America, which is why I haven't seen him for some years, but now he's on secondment to do a doctorate. He needed his thesis typing up and came to the agency. I couldn't believe it when he walked through the door.'

He'd believed her.

Morgan tossed the can onto the ground, giving it a vicious kick for good measure.

He'd *believed* her!

But then when she'd announced that she was leaving he'd realised just how blind he'd been.

Oh, she'd tried to pretend that nothing had happened. She'd offered several stumbling, clumsy explanations for her behaviour, but it had been obvious that she hadn't been telling the truth. The look on her face, the way her eyes hadn't been able to meet his but had slid away hastily, faint colour washing her cheeks, had all told their own tale.

In the end he hadn't been able to take any more.

'Tell the truth!' he'd demanded. 'Is there someone else?'

It was there in her face without a need for a word to be spoken. The sudden flare of relief in her eyes, the way she bit down sharply on her lower lip all told their own story.

'Yes,' she said slowly, almost sadly. 'Yes, there's someone else. Someone very, very special. Someone I can't bear to be without.'

And it didn't take much thought to work out just who the 'someone else' could be.

Pete.

Pride came to his aid then. The sort of pride that had always come to his aid as a child, when he had learned to show no response to his father's bullying, his mother's in-difference.

'Fine,' he said with a coolness that masked the way he really felt, the turbulent blend of anger and pain that threatened to explode inside him. 'In that case, the sooner you leave, the better.'

And he turned and walked away, not sparing her another glance.

But of course 'fine' hadn't described it at all, Morgan reflected, slamming his fist hard against the knotted trunk of the tree. 'Fine' had been a very long way from how he'd been feeling. So many times, on too many long and sleep-less nights like this one, he had reviewed the last months of their relationship, trying to see just what had gone wrong. Just what had Pete had to offer Ellie that he could not?

But he had never come up with *this*. Never come up with the possibility of something like Rosie.

And Rosie had to be Pete's. Unless...

Quickly he did the maths in his head. Ellie had been away eighteen months, and Rosie was... No chance, then, that she could be his. But Ellie must have got pregnant barely weeks after she'd left.

'You fool, Stafford!' he reproached himself furiously. 'You damn, stupid fool!'

He'd put Ellie's defection down to her youth. To the emo-tional impetuousness that had thrown her into his arms, de-claring her love for him barely a week after they had met. He had believed that she had simply transferred that emo-tion to Bedford, falling 'in love' with him with the same careless ease that she had experienced with Morgan.

He had never suspected there might be more to it.

He had come here in the first place because he'd been told that Pete was engaged to someone else. That the wed-ding was already planned for November. So, naturally, he'd been stunned when Ellie had flatly contradicted that report.

But perhaps Rosie's existence explained that. Ellie's pride would refuse to let her admit that the rat Bedford had got her pregnant and then deserted her for someone else. It would have helped if he'd known about the baby in the first place, then maybe he wouldn't have reacted so badly this afternoon, but better late than never. At least he knew now—and knowing gave him added leverage to use against Ellie.

He'd come here to find Ellie. What he'd planned to do then, he'd had no idea. He'd only known that he couldn't go on any longer enduring the emptiness that had been his existence since she'd left. And in the moment he'd first seen her again, he'd known why.

He still wanted this woman more than any other female he'd ever met. Still desired her with every part of his being. And he was determined to win her, no matter what it took.

Yawning, Morgan stretched widely, rubbing his hands across his face. She didn't know it yet, but Ellie had played right into his hands by letting him find out about Rosie. Bedford had clearly planned his life elsewhere, and, in spite of Ellie's protestations, it was obvious that money was tight. There would be things the little girl would need, things he could more than afford to provide. He could use the baby to get to the mother.

It was obvious that Ellie doted on Rosie. Taking an interest in the baby could only win him Brownie points where her parent was concerned. And the little girl was such a charmer that it shouldn't be too difficult to show that interest. It would also give him an excuse to be around Ellie, to try to win her round. Who knew? Perhaps even one day she might come round to thinking that her daughter needed a father.

Smiling to himself in satisfaction, he headed back to the cottage. For once, he might actually sleep what was left of the night away.

And then tomorrow he'd contact Ellie and make her an offer she couldn't refuse. He'd ring her first thing...

Ellie stood by the window in the farmhouse bedroom, staring out at the cool silver light of the moon in the night sky.

Well, early morning, actually. It had already been two when Rosie had woken, hot and restless as a result of the warmth of the night. It had taken a cool drink, a change of nappy, and several verses of a favourite lullaby to settle her back to sleep again, and for a time Ellie hadn't dared to move to go back to her own room for fear of disturbing her.

Not that she would sleep, she acknowledged gloomily. She hadn't even dozed off by the time she had heard the first faint sounds of the baby's waking. She'd spent the last couple of hours lying in bed, staring up at the ceiling, the scene with Morgan replaying over and over inside her head.

'Damn you to hell, Ellie—she's *yours*!'

The harsh words, and the blackly furious tone in which they had been flung at her, bit into her heart cruelly, like the lash of a whip, and she knew she would never forget the look on Morgan's face, the fury in his eyes, when he had turned on her.

'I—I can explain...' she tried, not knowing *how* she would manage any such thing.

It was impossible to impose any sort of coherence on the whirling mess of confusion that was all that was left of her brain. The only thing that was clear and uppermost in her mind was the one thing she knew she couldn't say.

Yes, Rosie's mine—but she's also yours! She's the baby you didn't want. The child you said would never be part of your life.

The temptation to fling the desperate words straight into his cold-eyed face was almost irresistible. In fact, she had actually opened her mouth to do so when Morgan forestalled her, cutting her off with an icy response.

'Don't bother!' he snapped, cold and curt, and so frighteningly distant that it was as if steel shutters had just come down inside his head, closing him off from her. 'You don't have to explain a thing.'

'But...'

'Ellie, there is nothing to explain.'

Each word was freezingly precise, making Ellie shudder in actual physical response as if they had been formed in letters of ice, falling cruelly onto her exposed skin.

Did he have to make it sound so absolute, so *final*? Ellie reflected miserably. Had he really been able to close the door on what they had had so completely and get on with his life without a single backward look? There was no trace of emotion in his voice, only a cold reasonableness that was somehow more agonising than the brutally angry verbal assault of his first response.

'What you've done since then, how you've lived your life, who you've been with, means nothing to me. It's entirely up to you who you've lived with, the men you've slept with...'

But that was too much.

'The *men*! How dare you? I'll have you know there was only one...'

'Apart from me,' Morgan finished for her when, horrified at what she had almost let slip, she swallowed down the dangerously revealing words. 'So Rosie is Pete's?'

'Rosie's *mine*!' Ellie hissed between clenched teeth, incapable, even to protect herself, of adding another lie to the one that panic had forced from her earlier. 'Mine and no one else's!'

One dark, arched brow lifted, cynically querying her overly vehement response.

'Don't you think that Bedford might have something to say on that matter?'

'No, I don't!' Ellie shook her head emphatically. 'I don't

think anyone has any right to express an opinion on this at all. Rosie and I are a unit, and what we do is nobody's business but ours.'

How different might things have been if she could have told him the truth, Ellie couldn't help wondering now as she turned back into the room, tears sheening her eyes as she looked down at her small daughter now fast asleep in her cot.

In her sleep, Rosie stirred, muttering faintly and flinging out a chubby arm, and Ellie bent to stroke the soft downy hair on her daughter's head.

'Would you like to get to know your daddy, sweetheart? Am I doing the right thing, keeping the two of you apart?'

From nowhere a memory winged its way into her thoughts. An image of her daughter and Morgan earlier that day in the moment that Rosie had leaned forward and patted her father softly on the cheek. The recollection slashed at her heart, tearing at her feelings so that she was unable to hold back a small moan of distress.

She would give the world to have that scene repeated. To let Morgan know that Rosie was his daughter and let her child know his father.

But hadn't Morgan surprised her today? A faint smile touched her lips at the thought of how he had tolerated Rosie using him for target practice, the good-natured way he had laughed off her use of a biscuit as an offensive weapon. Was it possible to build on that?

What if there was a way to ensure that the two of them—the man and the baby—spent more time together?

Smoothing the sheets around the small, sleeping form, Ellie came to a resolution. There was one way it could be done. If she agreed to take on the role of housekeeper as Morgan had requested and insisted on taking Rosie along, then perhaps, just perhaps, in time Morgan would get used to having the little girl around. He might even grow closer to her.

It was her only chance. She had to give it a try. She'd ring him first thing…

Morgan was just about to pick up the phone and dial the number of the farmhouse when, to his surprise, the sound of the bell shattered the quiet of the morning. With a surprised glance in the direction of the clock, registering the fact that it was only just eight, he snatched it up.

'Stafford.'

'Morgan?'

He recognised the voice instantly, his heart kicking in response to the low, slightly husky tones. If he closed his eyes he could almost imagine that she was there, next to him, whispering to him, as she used to do when they were in bed together, her mouth soft against his ear, the warmth of her breath…

'Morgan? It's Ellie.'

'I know.'

Hastily he collected his thoughts, forcing them back from the erotically charged path they had been following.

'What can I do for you?'

The struggle for control made his voice sound distant, coolly restrained. He could only be thankful that he hadn't been captured on a videophone where the screen would have revealed embarrassingly how easily and swiftly his body responded just to the sound of her voice.

'I've been thinking—about that housekeeping job…'

Was the woman a mind-reader? Another couple of seconds and he would have rung her about exactly the same thing.

'What about it?' Deliberately he kept his tone casual. 'If you're going to suggest that Dee—'

'No!' Ellie broke in hastily. 'No, I can see that you and Dee will never be able to work together. So—'

'Don't even think about suggesting anyone else, angel. I want you to do the job.'

'I know.'

Fingers clenching tight round the receiver, Ellie swallowed hard. Now that it had come to the point, she was close to losing her nerve. Last night she had been so very sure, so convinced that this had a chance of working. Now she was no longer so certain.

Twice she opened her mouth to speak; both times the words deserted her.

'Ellie?' Morgan's tone was sharp. 'Are you still there?'

'Yes, I'm here.'

'Then do you mind telling me what the point of this phone call is—if there is a point to it?'

'I'll do the job,' Ellie rushed in on him, suddenly terrified that he would lose patience and slam the phone down on her. 'The housekeeping job. I'll do it—but on one condition.'

'No conditions.' Concentrated and emphasised by the telephone receiver, the two words sounded brutally uncompromising, totally unmoveable.

'But I'll have to bring Rosie with me. She's too young to be left on her own, and I can't ask Nan to look after her. She has enough to do herself; I can't impose on her any more.'

The silence at the other end of the phone line was worrying, ominously long drawn out, stretching her nerves more with each second that ticked away.

'Morgan?' It was impossible to smooth the shake from her voice that revealed how important this was to her. 'Is that okay? She'll behave herself, I promise. I'll watch her all the time. I won't let her touch anything she shouldn't.'

Was he ever going to answer? If only she could see his

face and so grasp at some tiny clue as to what he was thinking.

'I want an answer, Morgan!'

She tried a different tack, not wanting to give him the chance to think he had the upper hand. She'd been too conciliatory, she saw now. If you were conciliatory with Morgan he walked all over you.

'It's me with Rosie or not at all. There's no other option on offer. Take it or leave it.'

'Then I'll take it,' Morgan drawled easily. 'Can you start today? The place is a tip.'

It was only when she put the phone down that Ellie realised how long she had been holding her breath, waiting for an answer. The hope of bringing her baby and the little girl's father together had meant so much to her that she knew it would have devastated her if he'd refused. But he hadn't said no.

Turning to head into the kitchen, she caught up her daughter from the rocking seat in which the baby was strapped and lifted her high.

'Your daddy's going to see us! Your daddy's going to see us!' she chanted, whirling her round until Rosie's face creased into a wide, delighted smile and she crowed with laughter.

'Oh, Rosie!' Shifting position, she brought the small, wriggling body close to her chest and hugged the baby tight. 'It's only a beginning—but at least it's something.'

At the other end of the phone line, in the hallway of Meadow Cottage, Morgan slowly replaced the receiver, a satisfied smile on his face.

He'd been prepared for an argument, for some difficulty in persuading Ellie to take up the position of housekeeper, but in the end she'd done all the work for him, and he had the bonus of getting to know Rosie too. He hadn't even had to ask. Things were going exactly the way he wanted, and right now Ellie was doing all the running.

If his luck held, he'd be able to put part two of his plan into operation much sooner than he had anticipated.

CHAPTER NINE

'YOU look tired.'

Morgan's greeting, with its note of concern, set Ellie's teeth on edge. She looked dreadful, and she knew it, and having him tell her so only added to her already ruffled mood. The day had begun hot and was now positively scorching and even the weight of the fine soft cotton of her loose green dress was almost unbearable, in spite of the fact that it was vee-necked and sleeveless.

Your daughter kept me awake half the night, she was tempted to declare, but discretion had her biting the foolish words back.

'Rosie didn't sleep well last night,' she said instead. 'And as a result, neither did I.'

'She seems peaceful enough now.' Morgan looked down at the little girl, fast asleep in her pushchair.

'Appearances can be very deceptive. Believe me, she wasn't at all peaceful at three this morning! I think she's cutting another tooth and that's what's making her so grizzly. I apologise in advance if she's difficult when she wakes up.'

Which was the last thing she needed. The whole point of bringing Rosie with her on these daily visits to Meadow Cottage was to get Morgan to like having the little girl around.

Up to now it seemed to have been working. In the five days since Ellie had been acting as Morgan's housekeeper, the baby had always been at her brightest and most delightful best during their visits. As well as that, she seemed to have developed a particular liking for her unknown father and crowed with delight whenever she saw him, holding out her arms to be held or picked up.

And a couple of times Morgan had actually obliged. Once when Ellie had had a struggle getting the pushchair into the cottage's narrow hallway he had come to help, manoeuvring it into the kitchen and parking it in a corner before unfastening Rosie's harness and lifting her out of the buggy. The memory of that moment still brought tears to Ellie's eyes with the recollection of the wide, brilliant beam on her daughter's face, and the way she had looked so right, so safe in the strong support of her father's arms.

Another time, when the baby had pulled herself up from her position on the floor using an armchair as a support, it had been Morgan who had spotted that she'd been about to overbalance and had stepped forward to catch her just in time.

It was a beginning. A small foundation on which Ellie hoped to build a better future.

'If she gets really bad, I'll take her back home so we don't disturb you.'

'Don't be silly, Ellie.' Morgan frowned. 'There'll be no need for that. I didn't plan on working this afternoon anyway. Thought I'd take an afternoon off.'

Ellie was none too sure how she felt about that. Over the past few days they had fallen into a sort of a routine. She would clean and tidy, prepare a meal, while Rosie played in the safety of the small playpen Morgan had unexpectedly provided from the very first morning. Most of the time Morgan shut himself away in the small gallery bedroom that he had set up as his workroom.

'Does this mean the book's going well?'

'Well enough.'

Which was a gross exaggeration, Morgan thought wryly. Oh, he went up to the gallery workroom every day when she arrived, switched on the computer and sat there, his attention supposedly fixed on the screen, occasionally pressing a couple of keys in an attempt to make it look as if he was doing something. But the truth was that he hadn't written a coherent word for days.

Instead every nerve was alert to the sounds in the rooms below, the sight of Ellie's slenderly curvaceous body as she went about her tasks, the clean sweet scent of her skin on the air. By the time she left he was burning with frustration, aching with need, and each day it got worse.

'But I thought I'd earned a break—and you have too. You look as if you need one anyway. I thought we could perhaps take Rosie out—go down to the beach.'

'I don't think so Morgan. I came here to do a job and if we go out I'll not finish what I had planned.'

'Oh, for heaven's sake!' Morgan exploded. 'How much work is there involved in keeping up a place this size? You could clean it from top to bottom in an hour—and that's including a ten-minute coffee break. You've been coming here every day for almost a week, Ellie. Just how much mess do you think I can make?'

'Not as much as you used to, that's for sure.' Ellie struggled for a smile and didn't quite manage it. 'In fact, I wouldn't even know you were writing a book if you hadn't told me. What's happened to the piles of scribbled notes, the first, the second drafts that you discard by screwing up the pages and tossing them into the bin—and usually miss?'

'The computer handles most of that,' Morgan growled, uncomfortably aware of the way that she had almost blown his cover. 'I can keep all the rough drafts on the hard disk and if I want to discard them it just takes a click of the mouse.'

'Then it's a pity you didn't have one when we were together,' Ellie retorted, hiding the sting of memory behind a mask of tartness. 'It would have made my life a lot easier.

So, if you're not working this afternoon would you like me to clean in the gallery?'

'No, I would not. I told you what I'd *like* is for us both to take the afternoon off together.'

She was tempted—more tempted than she would willingly admit, even to herself. But she couldn't give in to that appeal. To do so would be to lay herself open to dangers she didn't dare even contemplate. It was hard enough just coping with being in Morgan's company every day as it was. When she had agreed to this job, she hadn't reckoned on how much it would affect her to be with the man she loved and yet not able to show that love in any way.

'I don't think so.'

It twisted in his guts to watch the smile evaporate from her face, those golden eyes darken with distrust.

'Damn it, Ellie! I'm only offering a trip out, not threatening to sell you and the baby into slavery!'

'And *I'm* only saying that I came here to do a job and I'd be grateful if you'd let me get on with it!'

'You never used to be quite so houseproud when we lived together. Then I could easily tempt you away from the dusting...'

Oh, that was very definitely below the belt! Ellie winced inside at the memory of just *how* he had enticed her to leave the housework alone—not that she had needed much encouragement. But sometimes she had lingered deliberately, affecting an interest she'd been far from feeling just so that he would be forced to resort to even more seductive kisses, the sort of sensual caresses that had brought the hot blood rushing up under her skin, the whispered blandishments, hot, husky promises of the erotic pleasures he'd had in store for her.

Simply to remember them made her mouth dry, her thoughts swim in heady response.

'But in those days you weren't paying me for my services.' Once more she hid behind a pretence of severity in order to keep the necessary gulf of distance between them. 'Now you are and I'd prefer not to short-change you by not doing a good job. So if you'll just let me get on.'

'Be my guest.'

It was clipped and curt, exaggeratedly polite in a way that spoke volumes for the cold anger he was concealing behind the courtesy.

'But you're wrong, you know,' he tossed after her as she headed for the kitchen. 'In the past I did reward your services—only I paid you in kind.'

He paused just long enough to let the significance of that remark sink in. Long enough for Ellie to realise with a twist of shock in her heart that he too had been thinking of those long ago days. That, like her, he had been recalling the sensuous way he had distracted her from her tasks, the passionate delights that had so effectively put an end to any attempt at domestication.

'Any time you want to renegotiate your current contract,' he drawled provocatively, 'you only have to ask.'

Ellie refused to honour the suggestion with an answer, turning on her heel and marching away, not even giving him the satisfaction of showing that she had heard.

But she couldn't stop herself from thinking, and the thoughts that filled her head over the next hour were definitely X-rated.

Suddenly she seemed prone to hallucinations. The wood she wiped and polished developed the living warmth of Morgan's skin as she touched it. She could see his face reflected in the windows as she cleaned there, hear his voice in the sound of the breeze in the trees beyond. And the brilliant blue of the cloudless, sunlit sky was just a pale reflection of his eyes.

By the time she tried making the bed, only to find it impossible to resist picking up the pillows and pressing them to her face, inhaling deeply on the faint, lingering scent of his body, letting her lips touch the spot where his head had rested, she knew she was in deep trouble. Rosie or not, she couldn't work at the cottage any longer. Simply being here was stretching her nerves beyond endurance. Seeing Morgan every day was only feeding the hunger she had already been enduring; being able to see but not touch was more than she could bear.

Sinking wearily down onto the freshly made bed, she tried desperately to think of some way to tell him that wouldn't rouse his suspicions. It was not even a week since she had said that she would take up the housekeeping job. To back out so soon would only make him ask questions she knew she could never answer.

'Ellie?'

Morgan's voice sounded from the doorway behind her, startling her so that she jumped like a nervous cat.

'I thought you'd want to know—Rosie's waking up. Are you all right?' he added on a very different note, one as sharp as the narrow-eyed gaze that swept over her in swift assessment.

'I'm fine!' she managed automatically, though the dressing-table mirror in front of her told its own story, revealing the declaration for the lie it was.

Her face was pale, her eyes wide and dark, with shadows lying like bruises on the delicate skin underneath them. She looked dazed and only half awake, the struggle to drag her mind back into the present showing plainly on her drawn features.

He had been watching her for a while, standing silent and unnoticed in the doorway, wondering just what thoughts had been going through her mind. What had put that abstracted, faraway look on her face? Would he be a fool to think that because she was here, in his room, he might have some place in her thoughts?

Or...jealousy stabbed brutally as he forced himself to consider that maybe someone else—that rat Pete Bedford, for example—might be the one who occupied her thoughts.

'You don't look *fine*,' he growled, frowning in disapproval. 'In fact you look like hell.'

'Your flattery is overwhelming!' Ellie muttered, getting to her feet hastily as he moved into the room, coming swiftly to her side.

But movement was definitely a mistake. Just standing up made her head swim nastily. She felt faint and dizzy, her legs too weak to support her properly.

And what made matters so much worse was Morgan's physical presence so very close to her.

All night, when she'd had any sleep at all, she had been dreaming of him, heated, erotic dreams that had left her feeling wrung out and exhausted as if she'd never closed her eyes. All morning she'd been anticipating being here with him with a sense of expectancy that had quickened her pulse, warming her blood. And all afternoon she'd been imagining him with her, seeing him in her mind, picturing him wherever she turned.

And none of it had had the sheer mind-shattering potency of the reality. Not even her wildest, most erotic dreams could create a fantasy to match the impact of simply being able to see the lean, lithe body in another pair of those disreputably battered denim jeans and an immaculately white shirt. The shirt was worn loose, not tucked in at the waist because of the heat, and the top two or three buttons were left open revealing the strong column of Morgan's throat and just a suggestion of the crisp black hair that curled on his chest.

The warmth of the summer days had darkened his naturally olive skin so that the blue, blue eyes shone like brilliant sapphires in contrast to the warmth of his tan. A shaft of sunlight slanting through the small window fell straight onto the ebony sheen of his hair, making it gleam with vibrant health and life, and the clean, slightly musky scent of his body blended with a hint of a tangy cologne to assail her senses like some heady perfume.

She risked one brief glance into the depths of his eyes and saw his pupils darken, saw all the shimmering blue swallowed up by the black revealing a need that matched and outstripped her own. And felt her heart leap in uncontrollable response.

'Morgan...' she managed faintly.

'I'm here...'

Even Ellie couldn't have said whether the hand that fluttered out to take his was really in need of support or if she was simply giving in to an urge that she couldn't suppress. The need to touch, to feel, to actually know the slide of the warm satin of his skin under her fingertips, the strength of muscle and the hard power of bone as it adjusted to her grip, taking the weight of her slender body easily and without effort.

Ellie drew in a long, uneven breath and let it out again on a ragged, revealing sigh.

'Morgan...' she said again, but on a new and very different note.

Heavy eyelids fluttered upwards to allow her to look into his eyes, meeting the hooded, burning gaze. And in that moment something shivered between them. Something that asked a question and answered it without a word being said.

'Ellie, I...' Morgan began, but his words were interrupted as a sound impinged on their distracted consciousness, forcing itself to their attention.

Small at first, it was nevertheless enough to still them, hold them, listening intently. Then from the living room at the end of the short corridor the noise came again, more urgent this time, impatient, demanding, making its presence felt above the heavy pounding of their hearts.

'Rosie!'

Ellie's blurred gaze went to Morgan's face, seeing how his equally unfocussed eyes sharpened suddenly, losing the haze of desire, and snapping back to reality in a second.

'She's woken properly.'

The thought had barely time to form before Ellie was twisting out of Morgan's loosened hold, turning and running from the room just as the cry grew into a wailing crescendo of furious protest as Rosie came fully awake enough to realise that she had been abandoned.

'I'm coming, darling—coming!'

She reached her daughter's side just as the baby threw back her head and opened her mouth, ready for one final, outraged scream.

'Oh, darling, I'm *sorry*! Did you think I'd left you?'

Fingers clumsy with impatience and guilt, she struggled with the straps that held the baby safe, gratefully relinquishing the task when Morgan stepped forward and, his movements swift and efficient, unfastened them with easy speed.

Flashing him a swift smile of thanks, Ellie lifted the baby into her arms, holding her close and hugging her tightly, babbling a litany of reassurance as she stroked the downy head, gently touched the small, soft cheeks, flushed red with outrage.

'Mummy's here now, darling. I've got you safe. Everything's all right.'

It was only as her eyes met Morgan's over the baby's head that realisation hit home with a small, jolting kick of her heart.

Hearing her baby's wail, she had reacted on pure instinct, jolting out of the sensual trance that had gripped her, coming sharply back to earth in a second. Her love for Rosie, a love so primitive, so basic to her life, had overruled anything else, even the carnal spell Morgan had been weaving like a seductive spider, capturing her in its web.

But she hadn't been the only one.

At the moment that Rosie's cry had rung out, they had both frozen, then both *reacted*. When she had dashed out here, thinking only of the fact that her baby needed her, Morgan had been only a split second behind. The significance of that made her heart swell in delight, tears burning her eyes so that for a second or two she buried her face against the little girl's neck, hiding her response from the man who stood, silent and watchful, observing her every move.

'Is she okay?' he asked now, the rough edge to his voice snagging on Ellie's raw nerves.

She knew only too well what that rawness revealed. She was feeling exactly the same way herself, struggling with the gnawing ache of unappeased desire, the scream of protest of senses newly awoken only to be denied with cruel haste.

'She's fine,' she assured him gently. 'She just wasn't happy to find herself alone. Morgan...'

He knew what she was going to say. He could read it in her eyes, in the way they pleaded with him to understand. She was uncertain how he might behave, watching anxiously for clues to his response. And he knew how he had to react, in spite of the fact that it was the exact opposite of how he was feeling.

'It's okay,' he said gruffly, fighting a sharply uncomfortable battle with the clamouring demands of his senses. 'Your Rosie had to come first.'

'Your Rosie.' Ellie bit her lip hard against a cry of distress, some of the warm glow created by his earlier reaction ebbing away leaving an empty, hollow space deep inside.

Your Rosie. Morgan might have taken the first, wary steps along the road towards the future she dreamed of him having with his daughter, but it was only a beginning. They had a long, long way to go yet.

CHAPTER TEN

'WHAT about that trip out, now?'

Ellie's words slipped past defences breached by that sudden intense rush of emotion. She felt as if she had been drowning in fear and someone had suddenly and unexpectedly thrown her a lifeline, one she was determined to hang on to and use to the best of her ability.

'Rosie's wide awake and if I know her she'll be this way for hours yet. It would be a good idea to wear her out if I'm to have any chance at all of getting her to sleep tonight.'

If he said no, she didn't know how she would respond. Strangely enough, this small move seemed to matter so much more to her than the big, major thought of reconciliation. Perhaps it was because the thought of reconciliation was *too* big. It seemed too distant, impossible to achieve. But this was another tiny step in the two-steps-forwards, one-step-back process of getting Rosie and her father to learn to know each other better.

Morgan consulted his watch briefly.

'The worst of the sun has passed,' he said quietly. 'So there's less chance of you two getting burned. What about a trip to the beach?'

'That would be...' Ellie began but the words faded as she realised that the man's sapphire gaze was not on her but her daughter. Emotion knotted in her throat as she saw him look directly into the baby's face.

'Would you like that, monster?' he asked with a casual ease that tore at Ellie's overly vulnerable heart. 'Would you like to go on the sand? Maybe even dip your toes in the sea?'

For a long, long moment Rosie regarded her father with intense solemnity, matching blue gazes locking together, almost as if she were actually weighing up the matter and considering her answer.

'Bah!' she pronounced at last. 'Bah! Gah!'

'Seems the matter's decided.' Morgan laughed, the sudden lightening of his expression wiping years from his face in a second. 'The beach it is.'

'I'll get Rosie's hat...' Ellie muttered thickly, and fled hastily from the room before the tears that burned in her eyes gave away her feelings.

She couldn't continue this way any longer, Ellie decided a couple of hours later as she stood at the edge of the sea, letting the small waves tumble towards her bare pink toes, her daughter's laughter tickling her ear.

It was impossible to admit even to herself just how much she regretted the impulsive panic that had pushed her into the lie about the baby's age. If only she had spoken the truth then...

Then what?

Something caught in her throat so that she made a small choking sound, one she hastily covered up by turning it into a cough.

If she had told the truth she had no idea how Morgan would have reacted. She had feared that if he even suspected that Rosie might be his child he would have turned and walked out of her life without a backwards glance and she would have ruined every chance they might grow towards a reconciliation together.

But she hadn't told the truth and as a result Morgan was still here. But he was here for all the wrong reasons. He was here because he believed that Rosie was *not* his child. Because he thought she was Pete's baby, and so he didn't

need to put up any of the instinctive barriers he had against
the idea of having children of his own.

But the longer she allowed him to continue in that sort
of delusion, the harder it was going to be to reveal the truth
to him in the end.

Drawing a deep breath, she turned her bronze gaze to
where Morgan stood just a few feet away from her. Like
her, his feet were bare, their shoes kicked off at the edge
of the sand, and his jeans rolled up slightly to be clear of
the sea. The soft breeze was wafting the darkness of his hair
about his face as he skimmed flat stones along the surface
of the water, bouncing over the waves, and his narrowed
eyes were turned towards the horizon where the sun was
now slowly beginning its final descent of the day.

'Morgan...' she began hesitantly, struggling desperately
to find some way of beginning to tell him.

He couldn't go on this way any longer, Morgan told himself as he watched the last of the stones skim its way towards the horizon. He had come here to tell Ellie the truth
and had never managed it. With every day that passed he
felt the burden of that truth and the way it had affected their
past weighing ever more heavily on him. Something had to
break—and right now he felt as if it might actually be him.

He couldn't go on being with Ellie and keep his distance
like this. It was eating away inside him, ruining his work,
his sleep, his existence. He had only picked up the damn
stones and started throwing them into the waves in order to
distract himself from the enticing closeness of her body in
the loose green cotton dress. With the breeze swirling her
golden hair around the soft oval of her face, the sun gilding
the skin of her arms and throat, and her long legs and slender feet enticingly bare, she looked like some wild sea
nymph who had come on shore to beguile poor foolish mor-
tals back into her watery world where she would seduce
them...

Hell, no! Thinking of seduction was quite the wrong thing to do. For a couple of tormenting seconds he was actually tempted by the thought of wading out, waist high, into the chilly water. At least that way he might subdue the heated blood that pounded round his body, making him harden achingly.

He had to talk to her. It was make or break. All or nothing. Today something had to give or he would go quietly out of his mind.

'Ellie...'

Every thought in Ellie's head evaporated swiftly as he turned towards her and she realised that, low and hesitant as it had been, he hadn't heard her tentative approach.

'Want to walk?' he asked, his tone supremely casual, strangely belying the intense darkness of his eyes. There was a tautness about his shoulders that communicated the sort of tension that seemed to vibrate right through her until her toes curled in the damp sand.

'I'd like that.'

Her voice sounded rusty as if from ill use, her throat drying in the heat of her instinctive response to his closeness. She wanted to reach out and touch the tanned forearms exposed by the roughly pushed back sleeves of his shirt, smooth the tossed hair back from his high forehead.

'Is Rosie heavy?' he asked sharply, bringing her up hard against the realisation that unconsciously she had shifted the baby awkwardly in her arms, instinctively fighting the need to reach out to Morgan himself.

'No, she's fine.'

'I could carry her if you like.'

'Morgan, I said...'

'You don't want me to carry the kid—fine!'

Morgan's hands came out in a brusque slicing gesture, cutting off the topic of conversation with an abruptness that wrenched at Ellie's heart.

Impossible to explain how she felt. Impossible to tell him that she didn't feel she could cope with seeing the baby in his arms, not now, not when she was so supremely conscious of everything she was holding back.

'I...' she tried again but he was already moving away, his long strides covering the ground so that she had almost to run in order to catch up with him. 'Morgan, wait... Please!'

He slowed just enough to let her come level, but then he moved off again, kicking stones, shells out of the way, his eyes fixed on the skyline and the slowly setting sun, his attention apparently anywhere but on her.

If only he could find a way to begin. He couldn't just blurt it all out bluntly, baldly. There was too much ground to cover, and besides, he didn't know how much he dared risk saying. There was no way he could reveal the full truth until he knew how she felt about other things.

Start with something simple. Something innocuous.

'How are your parents these days?'

It was the last thing Ellie had expected. Morgan clearly had something on his mind, so when he had suggested a walk she had seen it as a lead-in to whatever he wanted to tell her. But she had anticipated something more significant than a chat about her family.

'They're fine,' she said, unable to keep the wariness out of her voice. It couldn't be this simple.

'Are they still at the same pub—the Elnett Arms, wasn't it?'

'That's right.'

She was still trying to work out just where this was leading.

'The last time I was there, they were planning on building up the catering side—did they go ahead with that?'

'Mmm—it's been very successful.'

Ellie could only pray he would believe her breathlessness

the result of having to trot in double-quick time in order to match the demanding pace he was setting. She didn't want him asking questions she couldn't hope to answer.

'I'm sure it has; your mother is a wonderful cook. And what about the Crazy Gang?'

'I presume you mean my brothers? Well, Rob's working with Mum and Dad now that the pub's been extended. Neil's doing a catering course at college, so I expect he'll go into the family business too. Dan's nicely established as an accountant, and he got engaged at Easter. He and Mary plan on marrying next spring. And of course William is still struggling with his schoolwork. He's just started his first year at sixth-form college...'

The last comment was a little unsteady. William, her youngest brother, had always suffered from a strong dose of hero-worship where Morgan was concerned, and he had been badly upset when she had told him that she and his hero were no longer a couple.

'I expect he'll go to university then.'

'If he gets the right grades.'

Morgan, just where is this going? she wanted to ask, but her nerve failed her and she resigned control of the conversation to him once more.

'Oh, I don't think there's much doubt about that. Will's a bright kid.'

'I'm sure you're right.' Ellie's smile was warm with a sisterly pride that even her edgy state of mind couldn't dim. 'He should pass his exams without any trouble.'

Abruptly Morgan came to a sudden halt, pushing his hands deep into his pockets as he stared out at the sea again.

'I always envied you your family,' he said sharply, making Ellie look at him in wide-eyed surprise.

'Envied?' This from a man who had declared he wanted no family of his own.

Morgan nodded sharply, his gaze still fixed on the horizon, jaw set into a hard line.

'I enjoyed the days we visited there, and that Christmas we spent with them made me realise what I'd been missing.'

Ellie knew she was gaping stupidly but she couldn't stop herself. Why was this happening? Why was Morgan saying all this *now*?

During the time they had been together, things that Morgan had let drop inadvertently had made her realise that, unlike her own happy, loving childhood, Morgan's own upbringing had been decidedly bleak. But he had stubbornly resisted her attempts to find out more, cutting her off sharply if she'd probed too deeply. So what had driven him to open up even to this small degree now?

'Do you mean a real family feeling?' she asked carefully.

'What's a real family feeling?' Morgan tossed back at her, his tone flat and unrevealing as his expression. 'The only family I knew was a mother who presented me with a succession of "uncles" so frequently that I never learned half their names, and a drunken sot who managed to kill himself by driving his car onto a level crossing in the path of an oncoming train.'

'Morgan...' Ellie choked, distress closing her throat. The words themselves were bad enough, but what made them all the more appalling was the ruthless, unnatural control he exerted over the way they were delivered. 'How old were you?'

'I'd just turned seven. I can't say it was much of a loss.'

The blue eyes defied her to turn what he was saying into a cause for sympathy.

'After all, he'd made it plain that he'd never wanted me born. He made sure I knew that he'd wanted my mother to have an abortion but she hadn't gone through with it—something she'd always regretted.'

'Oh, Morgan! I'm so—'

'No,' he cut in sharply. 'Don't say it. Don't say you're sorry. I don't want to hear it.'

'But why didn't you tell me?'

'It's in the past—over and done with. It wasn't relevant to us.'

Because he never intended to get caught in the trap that had closed round his father and mother. Was this what was behind Morgan's resolution never to have children? Perhaps he feared that, like both his parents, he was incapable of real love.

'But I wish I *had* known.'

She was looking back at their time together, painfully aware of the way that, secure and confident in her own family's love, she had rarely spared a thought for the fact that Morgan might have known a very different way of life.

'Why?'

If his defences had come down a moment earlier, now they had snapped firmly back into place, hard and impenetrable as ever.

'Would it have made a difference, angel? Would you have changed your mind, decided not to go off with the wonderful Pete if you'd known?'

In the face of such savage mockery, it took all of Ellie's courage to look into Morgan's face, and the icy fury she saw there almost destroyed her. Swallowing hard, she forced herself to admit the truth.

'No...' she whispered miserably, knowing she could say nothing else.

No matter what she had learned about him, in the same situation she would have had to make the same decision, no other one being possible—for Rosie's sake. But if she *had* known, then making that decision could only have been so much harder.

'No?'

Shockingly, Morgan seemed almost pleased, his echoing of her reply rich with sardonic satisfaction.

'That's a relief. For one appalling moment I thought you were going to say you'd have changed your mind. That's why I didn't tell you before. I wouldn't have wanted you to stay out of pity.'

'It wouldn't have been pity!' Her protest was sharp, indignant.

'No? Then what?'

Love. The word burned in her mind, so much so that she was afraid it might actually show in her eyes, that he could read it there, etched in letters of flame.

She would have stayed with Morgan out of love if she could have done. But she hadn't had that choice. And so, in a way, she had left him out of love too. Because her greatest fear had been that, like his father, Morgan would have wanted her to get rid of her baby. And knowing that it would have destroyed her, how it would have destroyed her love for him, if he had done that, she had run away rather than take the risk of it happening.

'I would have stayed if I could,' she murmured softly and saw his dark head swing round in shock.

'What did you say?' he demanded harshly.

'I…'

Words were whirling inside Ellie's head, broken, disjointed thoughts, none of which could form a complete whole, no matter how hard she tried. She didn't know what was safe to tell him; what would destroy her completely if she let it slip. She only knew she had to say *something*.

'Morgan… There's something you should know about Pete. We…we…'

'I know you're not together any more,' Morgan put in sharply. 'Do you think I'd be here if you were?'

'But you said you were here to research—'

'Ellie!'

Reaching out, Morgan took her face in his hands, the warmth of his palms along her cheeks as he turned her to face him, blue eyes blazing into her stunned golden ones. He'd vowed to tell her the truth and it seemed that the time had come to fulfil that vow.

'You must know that that was just a cover. That the real reason—the only reason I'm here is because I came looking for you.'

'You...? But *why*?'

'Why? Because I couldn't do anything else. Because ever since the day you walked out on me I haven't been able to get you out of my head, or fill the gap that you left behind. And I tried. God help me, I tried. But nothing worked. Then I found out you were here, and I was assured that you and Pete had split up, that you were on your own, and...'

He released her abruptly, spread his hands in a gesture of resigned defeat.

'I couldn't stay away. I had to see you one more time. To see if the old magic, the old passion was still there.'

'And was it?' Ellie whispered.

Looking deep into the darkness of his eyes, she read his answer there before his proud head dipped in a nod of acquiescence.

'I think you know the answer to that.'

She felt as if the world had suddenly tilted and swung round her. The distant horizon seemed to have moved, lying at an impossible, dizzying angle, one that made her feel as if the ground were no longer secure beneath her feet. The only things she felt sure of were the warm, solid weight of the baby in her arms, and the burning, intent gaze of the man before her.

'You know it was still there, Ellie. You know that I only have to look at you to want you, that no matter how hard I twist and turn, trying to get the hunger for you out of my mind, it's always there—you're always there.'

You're always there. Always there. Morgan's words seemed to sweep over her with all the irresistible power of the white-capped waves, washing aside all other thoughts.

Always there. It was impossible to hold out against the rush of response his declaration created. Impossible to hold back the delight that flooded through her.

'It's been the same for me,' she said huskily, her eyes still fixed on his, unable to look away. 'I've never been able to resist you.'

'Then don't,' he responded swiftly. 'Don't even try. Give in to what you're feeling, angel.'

Ellie's lips were dry and she wetted them nervously with her tongue, drawing that intent blue stare down to follow the tiny movement. Her own eyes were fixed on the softness of his mouth, the longing to know its feel against her own, to experience the delight of his kiss nagging like an aching bruise. *Give in to what you're feeling...*

'Morgan,' she croaked rawly, 'will you please stop talking and kiss me?'

His head went back slightly as if in shock, but then he smiled and the world turned on its axis again, making her head spin.

'My pleasure...' he murmured, one hand coming out, long fingers sliding under her chin, lifting her face to his.

Give in to what you're feeling... Wasn't it about time he followed his own advice? Time to forget about words and concentrate on actions instead.

But then his mouth took hers and all rational thought stopped. He was capable only of feeling, of knowing the hot race of his blood through his veins. Her lips were soft and yielding, opening sweetly under the demand of his, and as he slid his hands over her shoulders, down the smooth skin of her arms, she shuddered faintly and pressed closer to him. The roar of the waves echoed inside his head, growing in force and power until his head swam.

'Nah! Nahnah, nah!'

The baby's protesting interjection was a shriek in his ear. The next moment small, chubby hands clenched in his hair, pulling and twisting with painful effect.

'Rosie, no!'

Ellie's eyes were bright with consternation, her hands coming up to ease her daughter's clutching grasp, free the dark strands.

'Rosie, stop it! Morgan—I'm so sorry…'

'I guess she doesn't understand.' Morgan took a hasty step backwards out of reach of the waving fist. 'Perhaps she thinks I'm attacking you.'

'If anything, I think she's jealous…' Ellie's voice came and went weakly, finally cracking completely on the last word.

'Jealous?'

Morgan turned a questioning look on the little girl who answered the unspoken query by switching on her widest grin and holding out her arms wide, obviously pleading to be held by him.

And Morgan responded.

Ellie's heart stood still, her breath catching in her throat as he grinned suddenly and reached for the baby, hoisting her into his arms and then up high on his shoulder.

'Come on then, horror,' he said easily. 'It's time you stopped wearing your mother out. She's been carrying you all day.'

Morgan…

Twice Ellie opened her mouth to speak and both times nothing came out. She was incapable of anything beyond experiencing the rush of feeling that swamped her, biting her lip against the tears of joy she didn't dare let fall. She didn't even dare look Morgan in the face when he turned to her.

'I think it's time we went back to the cottage,' he said,

but the flames that burned in the darkness of his eyes promised more than just the simple words implied. 'Time we all had something to eat. Don't you think, Ellie?'

Holding the beaming baby securely with one hand, he held out the other to her, and, moving as if in a dream, Ellie took it, feeling the warm strength of his fingers close round hers with a sense of coming home.

'I think that's a very good idea,' she managed, incapable of saying anything more.

It was what she wasn't saying that troubled her. She knew that as well as answering the obvious question she was also agreeing to something else, something deeper and more important that lurked underneath the surface of what had been said.

That dark undercurrent swirled round her all the way home, thickening the air in the car until it was almost impossible to breathe. Each time Morgan moved she caught the warm scent of his body, mixed with the tang of the sea air, and the flex and play of the muscles in his arms and thighs as he controlled the powerful vehicle heated her blood to lava in her veins. She had never felt so tinglingly alive, so sensual, so deeply female in her life, the sensation like burning pins and needles making her stir restlessly in her seat at just the memory of Morgan's kiss and the promise it had communicated.

In her special seat in the back of the car, Rosie sang wordlessly, kicking her feet and waving her hands in the air as if conducting her own chorus. But for the first time ever since the baby had been born, even before the little girl had come into the world, Ellie felt a sense of separation from her daughter. She suddenly desperately wanted to be free to be herself, to be a woman, and to spend time with the man she loved.

So she was deeply grateful for the way that the little girl's energy sagged very quickly once they were back in the cottage, the blue eyes growing heavy almost as soon as she had been fed her tea, closing swiftly even as she lay on the changing mat being fastened into a clean nappy.

'She's just about asleep already,' she told Morgan as she lifted the baby from the mat and adjusted her disordered clothing.

Silently he came and took the limp little body from her arms, laying Rosie gently in the pushchair and adjusting it so that she could lie flat. Then still without a word he held out a hand to Ellie herself, helping her up from where she knelt on the floor, drawing her to her feet so that she stood against him, her body touching his at chest and hip and thigh.

She was barely upright, still finding her balance, when his dark head bent and his mouth claimed hers.

Immediately it was as if he had set a lighted match to the blue touchpaper of a fizzing firework, triggering a thousand brilliant explosions of desire, a myriad pulsing reactions running along every nerve making her shiver in response. Her head was swimming, her heart beating in double-quick time. It was impossible to hold back the instinctive moan of pleasure, impossible not to sigh her delight straight into his mouth.

'Do you know how much I've wanted that?' Morgan questioned harshly against her lips. 'How hard it's been to have you here, day after day, and not be able to touch you or kiss you?'

She couldn't form any words to answer him. Could only nod her understanding of exactly what he meant. Because she understood so well—too well for comfort. Hadn't she felt that way too? Hadn't she endured those long days of sensual deprivation and gone home in a fever of frustration, her body aching restlessly?

But then she looked into Morgan's eyes once more and saw them change. Saw the darkness envelop the blue, the flicker of need changing to the yellow flames of passion in the space of a heartbeat. And something of the ache of memory that had attacked her heart eased, erased by a growing heat of response.

'But this is just the beginning, Ellie,' Morgan told her harshly, his gaze locking with hers and holding it transfixed, unable to look away. 'Our time will come, and then nothing in the world can stand between us.'

It was a statement of intent, a promise and a threat all rolled into one, and Ellie knew that when he was in the mood there was no way at all that she could fight him.

Not that she wanted to fight. She wouldn't even try to resist, no matter how much her sense of self-protection might scream at her that that was the wise, the only sensible way. Where Morgan was concerned she didn't feel wise or sensible, and she never would. From the day they had met, from the moment he had first kissed her, she had belonged to this man, body, heart and soul, and there was nothing she could ever do to change that.

Suddenly Morgan moved, closing both hands over the tops of her arms, holding her prisoner. It was now or never. He had to have an answer. Knew he couldn't go on any longer without one.

'Ellie,' he said sharply, almost roughly. 'Don't go home tonight. Stay here with me.'

She knew what her answer would be as soon as he spoke. Knew there was only one thing she could say. But there weren't just the two of them to consider any more, and if there was ever to be any hope of a future he had to accept that.

But he was there before her, answering her question before it was spoken.

'You and Rosie, of course. If we can sort out somewhere for her to sleep.'

The answer to that was easy. She had known it all along, and had only been waiting for him to ask.

'There's a travel cot in the cupboard under the stairs. We keep it there for families with small babies who rent out the cottage.'

Someone who knew Morgan less well might not have noticed the faint flicker of response in those darkened eyes, the way the tension in the broad, straight shoulders eased just a fraction, betraying his inner feelings. But Ellie was hypersensitive to everything about him and experience taught her how to read the signs he almost disguised.

'So,' he said, aiming for a throwaway indifference and missing it by a mile, 'do I take it you're staying?'

Ellie drew in a deep breath, and let it go again on a sigh. She felt absolutely petrified, yet at the same time crazily, wildly exhilarated. The sensation that gripped her had to be something like the experience of jumping out of a high-flying plane at the beginning of your first ever parachute jump. Whatever happened, life would never be the same again.

But it was a risk she wanted to take.

'Yes, Morgan,' she said softly. 'I'm staying.'

CHAPTER ELEVEN

'ROSIE'S asleep.'

Ellie stood in the doorway of the kitchen, watching as Morgan took the foil from a bottle of wine before reaching for the corkscrew.

'As I thought, she was worn out. She barely had time to listen to the lullaby before she was well away.'

What *was* he doing? When she had left her baby daughter asleep in the travel cot and come to find him, the last thing she had expected was this cool distance, this almost calculated indifference.

And it was not what she needed. What she wanted was to be taken into his arms as soon as she appeared. She wanted to be kissed senseless; to be caressed until her body was a quivering jelly, her mind just a scream of need. She wanted to rediscover that hungry passion that had gripped her on the day of Morgan's arrival at the cottage and let it swamp her thoughts to the exclusion of everything else.

But Morgan showed no sign of even wanting to come close, let alone kiss her and caress her into oblivion. Instead he was concentrating on pouring two glasses of wine with an unbelievable care, almost as if his life depended on each glass containing exactly the same amount.

'I doubt if she'll stir before morning... A thunderstorm wouldn't disturb her,' she tried again.

Morgan simply nodded silently, setting the bottle aside and picking up a glass which he held out to her.

'Drink?' he enquired casually, sparking off a flare of exasperated, frustrated temper.

'No, I do not want a drink, Morgan!'

'I thought it might relax you.'

'I don't need relaxing! I'm perfectly at ease.'

Or, rather, she had been until a moment ago when he had started this unexpected prevaricating.

'And I don't want any artificial stimulants either—that's not what I need. I want…'

Her voice failed her as Morgan lifted his own glass and took a long swallow of the rich ruby wine.

'I want…'

'You want…' Morgan echoed sardonically. 'That's the thing, angel. Tell me, exactly what do you want? Why, precisely, are you here?'

What the hell was up with him?

Morgan had been asking himself the question ever since Ellie had taken the baby away to have her bath and get her ready for bed. Why, when what he wanted most in all the world, when the sole reason for his being here, in Cornwall, at all, was there almost in his grasp, and all he had to do was to reach out and take it, had he suddenly been plagued by an attack of severe second thoughts?

Why had he suddenly felt the need to put a distance between himself and this woman when the truth was that his body had been in a state of burning need every second of the time he had been with her? Why did he not simply reach for her and kiss them both senseless, plunging into the sensuality he craved as he might dive head first into icy water, submerging himself totally until he was incapable of thought?

Because he didn't trust that sensuality.

That was the heart of the problem. He'd been there before, got caught that way in the past, and it had not been enough. He'd fallen head over heels for Ellie, rushed into a relationship with her on the crest of the burning waves of the passion they'd both shared, and then, just as he had begun to feel secure enough to risk more, it had all fallen apart.

'I don't understand.'

Ellie's voice dragged him out of thoughts of the past, forcing him to concentrate on the present.

'You know very well why I'm here.'

Had she read things all wrong? Had he really not been in the grip of the same sensual enslavement that had gripped her all day? Had that fizzing excitement, that growing hunger been hers and hers alone and not the mutual need she had believed they shared?

'You asked me to stay. You said you wanted... Morgan, what is it? Don't you...' her voice cracked on the words '...don't you want me any more?'

'Want you?'

For a second Morgan closed his eyes against the appeal in her golden gaze, a faint groan escaping him.

'Not want you? Oh, Ellie!'

'Then why...? Is it because you don't think that Pete and I—?'

'It's got nothing to do with Pete!'

Nothing to do with Pete and everything to do with Ellie herself. Ellie, whose impassioned declarations of love had left those soft lips so easily in the past, who had spoken of futures and for ever so easily and yet had run off after new excitement almost before the sound of those ardent protestations had even died away.

'Because if it has, let me assure you. Pete isn't part of my life in any way at all. He never—'

'I said it had nothing to do with Pete!' Hard-edged with fury, the words slashed through her stumbling attempt at explanation. 'Don't bring that man's name into this. This is just you and me.'

Which made it easy, Ellie thought, managing a smile. She didn't know what barriers he had suddenly decided to erect around himself, but she was determined to break through them.

'And that's just the way I want it, Morgan. This is our time—just you and me, and no one else.'

Not even Rosie, she told herself, refusing to listen when a small voice of caution warned her that she would do better to try to tell him the truth now, before things went too far. She wanted this, *needed* it. This time was for her as a woman, time with her man, and she wanted nothing else to intrude. If there were any consequences she would face them—but later.

Fired with new determination, she took a step forward into the room and knew immediately from the way he watched her, that brilliant, unblinking gaze fixed on her face, that deep down, underneath the façade he had thrown up, he was feeling exactly the same way.

'Just you and me,' she repeated, a husky note of longing creeping into her voice. 'That's all I want—all I need right now.'

She held his narrowed gaze, smiling straight into the darkness of his eyes and caught the flare of response he couldn't control.

'This is for us, Morgan. Just for us. Nothing else matters and nothing can spoil it. So tell me what you want and you can have it. You only have to ask...'

You only have to ask.

She stood there before him, looking like all his fantasies come true and said *that*! With the warmth of the sun still lingering on her cheeks, the tumbled honey gold of her hair falling softly around her shoulders, and the amber-coloured eyes deepened to smoky bronze, she looked as if she had just stepped out of one of his hottest, his wildest erotic dreams.

His body tightened in an instant, the control he had been trying to exert slipping from him at once. His heart-rate quickened, leaping into overdrive between one breath and the next, driving rational thought before it instantly. Desire was like a fever in his blood, fighting a battle with the reservations, the doubts he had been struggling with moments before.

And desire won. To hell with the thought of what tomorrow might bring. So what if this was only passion, nothing more than lust, on either part? It was still communication at its most basic. And right now it was what he needed, what his hungry body cried out for.

'I want...'

The wineglass was slammed down on the workshop with a disturbing crash as Morgan swung round to face her fully at last.

'You know what I want. Come here,' he commanded, his voice raw and husky, his hand coming out in a gesture of supreme arrogance, motioning her towards him.

She didn't hesitate, moving forward swiftly, her eyes fixed on his. Putting her hand into his outstretched one, she felt his strong fingers close around it, holding her tight.

'And you know what I want,' she said firmly. 'You know why I'm here.'

Standing on tiptoe, she reached up and brushed her lips against his, just once, then dodged away again.

'I want this...' she said, a laugh escaping a little breathlessly as she sensed his immediate response, saw the burning look he turned on her, heard his swiftly indrawn breath. 'And this...'

This time the kiss was slower, lingering softly until she felt his lips open under the gentle pressure, knew the silken stroke of the tip of his tongue along her mouth.

'And *this*...'

Her free hand crept up around his neck, sliding into the dark silk of his hair, shaping itself to the muscle and bone of the back of his skull. With gently insistent pressure she brought his head down to hers, deepening the kiss until it was pure enticement, total provocation and sensual invitation all in one.

Beneath her lips she heard Morgan sigh, the sound blending into a groan of surrender as she was hauled up close against him, crushed against the hard wall of his chest. A tiny adjustment of his stance, the angle of his head, altered their positions subtly, changing the balance of power.

Morgan was now very definitely the one in control. It was his mouth that tormented hers, his grip that held her still, his hand in the small of her back that arranged her slender frame exactly to his liking. And what he liked was to have her slim hips cradled hard against his pelvis so that she was tormentingly, burningly aware of the heated, swollen evidence of the swiftness and strength of his response.

'So now do you know what I mean?' she managed, the words coming and going in a breathy, patchy way as she felt her own excitement rise to meet and match his. 'Do you know how I feel? What you do to me?'

'Oh, I know.'

Morgan's response was low and deep-toned, husky with a vocal echo of the physical need she knew was burning through him.

'Oh, Ellie, I *know*.'

Strong fingers tightened on her hand, crushing her fingers, his other arm coming round her waist, supporting her as she swayed against him, the sound of his voice affecting her like the intoxicating rush of some potent wine. Against her breasts was the solid power of his chest, the heavy, sensuous beat of his heart setting up an echo inside her own body.

'I know what you're feeling because I'm going through it too. You're there in my mind from the moment I wake until I fall asleep at the end of the day. And even then I'm not free of you. You come to me in my dreams and you

offer me all I've ever wanted. You're warm and willing—
so willing…'

'I dream of you too…'

She couldn't hold back the words, couldn't have suppressed them if her life had depended on it. They had been
building up inside her head like water behind a dam and as
soon as she opened her mouth they came pouring out, gathering speed with each second, tumbling over each other in
their haste to be spoken.

'I dream of how it used to be to be in your arms, in your
bed. I dream of your kisses—of your touch. Oh, Morgan!'

It was a cry of longing, of hunger.

'Morgan, I want you to kiss me *so much*!'

Had she even said the words out loud or just heard the
expression of her need inside her head? She didn't know,
but it didn't matter anyway because Morgan was there before her, his mouth taking hers even as she spoke, his lips
crushing her softness with a hungry passion that matched
her own. Without hesitation she opened herself to him, letting his tongue slide into the warm, moist interior, meeting
the sensuous invasion with an eager response that made him
groan aloud in a mixture of surrender and delight.

His hands were hot against her back, his touch tracing
paths of fire over the exposed skin of her arms and her neck,
until she writhed in delighted response. Moving higher, the
strong fingers clenched in her hair, holding her head at just
the right angle so that he could deepen the kiss, dominate
her mouth completely.

She felt as if she was swooning again—this time not from
weakness, but from the sheer force of the blaze of desire
that swamped her. There was no room for thought inside
her head, only hunger and the yearning need that was too
fierce to be controlled.

Her heart raced, her breasts ached for his touch and heat
pooled between her legs, making her move restlessly against

the heat and hardness of him, bringing a choking cry from his throat.

'Ellie, if you knew how much I've wanted to do this… How much I ached to hold you, kiss you…'

Those restless hands were pushing at the neck of her dress, his thumb resting against the spot where a frantic, erratic pulse beat wildly while the long, probing fingers reached down to the soft curves of the upper slopes of her breasts.

'I want to touch you, really touch you…see you naked…'

'Yes!' Her response was every bit as urgent as his. 'Yes, Morgan, yes.'

Her feet were swung from the ground as he lifted her bodily into his arms, shouldering the door open to carry her through the living room where Rosie slept peacefully, down the corridor to the small back bedroom. There he let her slide to the floor, every shivering inch of her making contact with the heat and hardness of him before his arm clamped round her waist again, strong fingers twisting in her hair, holding her mouth captive under his.

His tongue tormented her, touching, tasting, tangling with hers, creating a seductive dance that set her senses alight, making her writhe against him.

'More…' It was a moan of surrender, mixed with hungry demand when he finally lifted his head, drawing in a ragged, uneven breath. 'More!'

'More?'

A touch of laughter lightened the question, glinting wickedly in his eyes as he looked down into her flushed and uplifted face.

'More of what, my angel? More of this…'

Butterfly kisses danced their way down her face, touching briefly on each brow, her eyelids, the tip of her nose.

'Or this?'

The caressing mouth moved lower, along the fine line of

her jaw, down her throat, teeth lightly grazing the delicate skin, his tongue tracing erotic patterns around the hollow at the start of her shoulder.

'Or this?'

She hadn't even felt his hand find the zip at the back of her dress and slide it downwards, so the first she knew was when he pushed the green straps down her arms, following the path with his caresses, his kisses, raising tingling goose-bumps of reaction wherever he touched. Sighing his name out loud, Ellie moved slightly, lowering her hands so that the fine material whispered downwards over her body, falling away and pooling on the polished wooden floor at her feet.

The front fastening clasp of the pale peach bra was swiftly dispensed with, the satin cups falling easily away to expose the generous curves of her breasts to his hungry eyes and hands. Hands that moved to cup and lift the soft weight, thumbs centring on the straining nipples, circling over them over and over again, bringing such agonising pleasure that she moaned aloud at the delight of it.

'Morgan...'

It was a choking cry of surrender, of total submission to the feeling he could create in her by his touch, his kisses. Flinging her head back, she arched her spine, instinctively bringing the peaks of her breasts closer to him, offering herself to him in mute demand for more. And Morgan sensed exactly what she wanted, lowering his dark head until the heat of his mouth burned against the creamy flesh. He still held her in the hard warmth of his palms, while his lips moved slowly down, down until at last they closed over the hardness of one pink nub.

For a second the slick heat of his tongue circled the delicate skin, bringing soft, unformed sounds of pleasure from Ellie's throat, but then the caress changed to a fierce demand, closing tightly, suckling strongly, sending stinging electrical currents burning a path downwards, directly to the innermost point between her thighs.

'Please... Oh, please... Oh, please...'

It was a litany of urgency, of need, muttered over and over again in uncontrollable response to the wild sensations surging through her. And as she abandoned all control, her hands tugging at the buttons on his shirt, wrenching them open, her eyes closing in an attempt to intensify and prolong her pleasure, she felt his passion grow to match her own, his breathing rasping heavily, his skin burning beneath her touch.

'Steady...Ellie...steady.'

It was a raw-voiced note of warning as her impatient hands dropped to the waist of his jeans, tugging clumsily at the leather belt that fastened them.

'I don't feel steady!' she declared defiantly. 'Steady is the last thing I want, I—Oh!'

The words broke off on an exclamation of surprise as, taking her unawares, Morgan lifted her again and swung her towards the bed, dropping her onto the crisp white quilt and coming down swiftly beside her.

'The last thing you want, hmm?' he questioned, the blend of amusement and impatience roughening the edges of his words. 'Well, that suits me...'

Demanding fingers wrenched the small scrap of satin and lace that was her only remaining covering from her hungrily trembling body. His own clothes followed just as swiftly, and, lost in the heated pleasure of flesh on flesh, Ellie couldn't stop herself from writhing closer, pressing the stinging tips of her breasts against the dusting of hair on his chest, moving the softness of her lower body against the heated power of his erection.

'Ellie...' This time the warning was more pronounced. 'If you do that, I won't be able to control myself.'

'Then don't control yourself,' she tossed back at him,

increasing the wanton pressure deliberately so that he groaned aloud. 'This isn't a time for control.'

'Oh, isn't it?'

Something fiendish glinted in the blazing blue eyes, flashing a momentary warning. But before she had time to do more than register it, to wonder exactly what he had in mind, she was grabbed around the waist and tumbled onto her back on the bed, Morgan coming with her, up and over her, to hold her imprisoned against the pillows.

'I'll show you control,' he muttered, capturing both her wandering hands in one of his and forcing them above her head, clasping strong fingers hard around both wrists so that she could not escape.

It was as much an assault on his senses as on hers. With every touch, every kiss, every tantalising exploration of the most intimate pleasure spots on her body, his own need grew stronger, wilder, closer to the edge.

When she moaned her delight and sighed his name it was all he could do not to give in to the urge to forget restraint, to bury his clamouring body in the heat and tightness of hers, to give in once and for all to the fever that had him in its grip.

But he had promised control and, though there were times that he had to clench his teeth against the groan of surrender that almost escaped him, somehow he managed to hold himself back from the moment of final possession until she was pleading with him, begging him to end the delightful torment.

Ellie felt as if her whole body were on fire. There wasn't an inch of her skin that hadn't been kissed, stroked, licked or suckled into throbbing arousal. Some particular tender spots were so on fire that it was a sensation on the very edge between pleasure and pain, so much so that she couldn't take it any more.

'Morgan...' she gasped, reaching for his hands, stilling

their tormenting journey down to where the centre of her need pulsed between her legs. 'No more—please—I want you! I want you inside me—I want you to love me properly.'

'Oh, I'll love you *properly* all right,' was the muttered response as with a fierce sexual urgency he parted her smooth thighs and slid his own muscular, hair-roughened ones into the space he had made. 'I'll love you so thoroughly, so completely that you'll think you've never been loved before by anyone—anyone at all.'

And with a thick, rough sound of triumph deep in his throat he thrust his powerful body into hers, bringing his mouth down hard on her lips to capture and swallow up the high, keening cry of delight she made as she abandoned herself to his possession.

It was hard and hot and fast. Their breathing was heavy, raw, ragged, their skin slick with the sweat of mutual desire. Each movement took them deeper, further, higher, bodies moving in perfect unison, tightening each nerve, stretching each delight until they reached the final peak. The point from where there was nowhere further to go only over the final, glorious precipice, tumbling, whirling, splintering over the edge, and into a mindless oblivion of completion.

CHAPTER TWELVE

THE sun streaming through the lace curtained window and falling onto her face was what woke Ellie the next morning.

Yawning deeply, she stretched with luxurious contentment, enjoying the sensation of warmth, then froze suddenly as realisation hit home belatedly.

She wasn't at the farmhouse having an unexpectedly late lie-in because Rosie had slept better than usual. She was at the cottage where she and Morgan had spent the night locked in each other's arms. Memories of the night flooded her mind, her skin colouring just to think of it. Her whole body ached as she moved and there were one or two faintly tender spots, the feel of which reminded her sharply of Morgan's particularly intimate attentions.

'Morgan?'

Cautiously she opened her eyes and looked around, finding the bed beside her and the rest of the room totally empty and silent.

And emptiness and silence were not what she wanted. Last night she had been so very sure that what she'd been doing had been right, but now, in the clear light of day, things looked very different.

Hadn't she been guilty of rushing in blindly, seeing only what she'd wanted to see, not really thinking at all? In all of the long, passion-drenched night Morgan had never spoken a word of love or anything close to it. In fact, he had rarely spoken at all, but had let his body, his hands and his lips communicate for him. And what his lovemaking had said was that he desired her, he wanted her physically with a hunger and an urgency that still made her head swim to think of it—but was there anything more than that?

Because there had to be more. If she was to do more than dream of any sort of a future with Morgan. If she was to hope to rebuild their relationship, to tell him the truth about Rosie...

Rosie!

Every last trace of lazy relaxation fled as she suddenly registered just what the brightness and the warmth of the sun should have told her as soon as she had woken.

It was late in the morning, and surely by now her daughter must have woken.

A swift glance at her watch told the full truth of the matter. On a normal morning Rosie would have been up, dressed—and *fed* by now! How could she have slept so long? And where was the baby? Where was Morgan, too?

Even as the question formed in her head she was flinging back the quilt and leaping out of bed. A navy towelling robe lay across a chair and she snatched it, pushing her arms into the sleeves as she ran, and tightly belting it round her slim waist.

Her bare feet made no sound on the carpeted floor and so as she came close to the half open door of the living room she caught the faint sounds of movement beyond. Movement, and the low, muted tones of Morgan's voice and a baby's laughter.

Relief slowed her rushing footsteps as, assailed by a whole new set of very different sensations, her heart seeming to beat high up in her throat, she paused, gently pushing the door an inch or two further open, and peeped round.

'You want another biscuit?'

It was Morgan's voice, low and unexpectedly soft, a hint of laughter warming it in a way that had Ellie biting down hard on her lower lip in order to hold back her cry of reaction.

'I don't know where you're putting all this food, monster. You're such a tiny scrap... Oh, all right! Just one... But don't tell your mum because I'm sure I'm feeding you all the wrong stuff.'

He was sitting in one of the deep red armchairs, his back to the door so that he was unaware of her presence. She could see the glossy dark hair, the broad shoulders under a crisp navy tee shirt. His long legs were stretched out in front of him, and sitting right by his left foot, a biscuit in her hand, an array of toys scattered round her, her face upturned and a look of complete bliss on her little face, was Rosie.

'Oh...'

Ellie clamped a hand over her mouth as tears blurred her vision. She didn't want to alert either of them to her presence in the slightest way. She just wanted to stay here unobserved and watch, holding her breath for fear that if she made a sound the scene might shatter and prove to be a total illusion.

'No—not the drum, Rosie...'

Seeing the baby reach for the instrument lying nearby, Morgan moved hastily, lifting a couple of brightly coloured plastic bricks and holding them out to distract her.

'We don't want to wake your mum, do we?'

'Doh!'

Rosie grabbed at one of the bricks, banging it enthusiastically against Morgan's leg for a second then throwing it away, clutching instead at the material of his jeans, and pulling herself upwards. Balancing precariously on not-quite-steady feet, she held on tightly, supporting herself with clinging hands on the man's knee as she bounced up and down delightedly.

'Doh! Doh! Da, da, dadadada!'

Ellie's heart clenched sharply. For a while now Rosie had been stringing syllables together but why should she choose that particular combination, one she'd never used before, just at this moment?

'Sorry, horrible. You've got the wrong guy.' Was that a note of regret in the quiet voice? 'That's Pete Bedford's job—not that—'

Morgan broke off sharply and a bubble of laughter rose up in Ellie's throat. She knew only too well what her daughter's sudden stillness, the red-faced grimace meant, and a second later it was clear that Morgan had realised too.

'Rosie!' he exclaimed in pained exasperation. 'I just put that nappy on!'

Perhaps now was the moment to come to his rescue, Ellie thought, but something held her back, just for a little longer. She wanted to see how Morgan handled this development.

Maybe...just maybe...the hope was like a refrain in her head.

She had decided. She *would* tell him. She had to. There was no other way forward. No hope of any future if she didn't. And if he walked away from them, it would be his loss.

'Rosie, you monster! And after the struggle I had to get this on in the first place!'

Morgan's groan of protest made the laughter bubble again. Peering round the door, she saw that the baby was now lying on the plastic changing mat, her legs waving wildly in the air, and Morgan knelt on the floor beside her, wipes, cream and disposables close at hand. Perhaps she should take pity on him...

Just one minute more. Smiling to herself, she waited and watched. But that minute was her undoing, shattering her mood completely.

'You can laugh all you want,' Morgan said, looking down into the baby's face while Rosie grinned up at him. 'But you're not going to faze me, lady. I have too much at stake. You see you...'

One long finger tickled the baby's tummy very gently, making her giggle and writhe in delight.

'Are my ace card. Your mummy dotes on you—and I want your mummy. I want her right where she was last night, in my bed. And I decided a while ago that if being nice to you, monster, was what it took, then that was the way to go. If nights like last night are the result, I reckon I can put up with…'

But Ellie had heard enough. Her world was spinning round her, her weak, foolish, fragile dreams, dreams so recently formed, so briefly acknowledged, splintering into tiny irreparable pieces. Her heart hurt as if one of those splinters had actually pierced it, wounding her terribly. His words beat against her skull, battering at her thoughts until she thought she might scream aloud in pain.

She couldn't stay. Couldn't risk being seen. Couldn't face Morgan—or Rosie—again until she had had some time to gather her thoughts. Clutching the robe around her as if it might hold the shattered pieces of her desolated soul together, she fled down the corridor to the sanctuary of the bedroom.

Morgan had set out to seduce her. He had made it plain that that was what he had wanted from the start. That he still desired her, wanted her physically, but with no emotional commitment. She'd turned that down, but she should have known that Morgan never took no for an answer. He always had some other plan up his sleeve.

And this time the plan had been Rosie. Knowing how much she adored the little girl, he had coldly, callously set out to use that love to his own advantage. He had decided that if he was nice to the daughter, if he put aside his own unwillingness to have children and pretended to like the little girl, then the mother's heart would melt.

And it had worked, hadn't it? Oh, God, it had worked! Huddled on the bed, Ellie could only stare, dry-eyed, at the floor, too distraught, too damaged, even to be capable of tears.

She had fallen straight into Morgan's carefully baited trap—and straight into his bed. Because, with a terrible irony, there had been one further advantage that he possessed, one that even his scheming mind wasn't capable of thinking up. He had never dreamed that fate had already weighted the result on his side because she was predisposed to believe he might care for Rosie, because she so desperately wanted him to love not just any baby, but his *daughter*.

'You're very quiet.'

Morgan studied Ellie's face as she walked silently beside him, trying to understand her mood. She'd been strangely distant and unapproachable ever since she had emerged from the bedroom late this morning.

'I don't feel like talking.'

'That much is blatantly obvious.'

At the start he'd been prepared for her to feel awkward about the way she'd fallen into his arms last night. Be honest—he'd expected second thoughts, so he hadn't been too concerned when she'd obviously found it difficult to face the 'morning after' moment, even after she'd lingered in the shower for far longer than anyone actually needed to get clean.

So he'd tried to give her space, offering only a casual greeting, a cup of coffee, thinking she'd come round eventually. But she'd spurned the coffee, insisted on going home straight away. She'd not even listened to his suggestions of lunch, another trip out, but had marched round the cottage, snatching up Rosie's clothes, the toys, bundling the baby into the pushchair in spite of the little girl's furious protests.

She'd have left then and there without even a kiss goodbye if he hadn't insisted on walking along with her. And she had made it plain that his company wasn't welcome, wouldn't so much as let him push the buggy, but had snatched it away from him when he'd simply put a hand on it.

'You certainly got out of the wrong side of the bed this morning,' he growled. Her bad temper was starting to rub off on him.

'It's the fact that I ever got into it that's bothering me.'

So he was right about the second thoughts. Typical Ellie. Act first and think later. Glancing at her pale, set face, he felt a twist of conscience at the sight of the lack of colour, the shadows lying like bruises under her eyes. It had been quite a night.

'Are you still tired?'

'And what is that supposed to mean?' Ellie snapped, her hands clenching over the handles of the baby buggy. 'Are you suggesting that last night wore me out? Well, perhaps I don't have your sexual stamina...'

'What the hell are you on about now?'

'I would have thought it was obvious.'

She wouldn't even look at him, just marched straight ahead, her face firmly turned away, eyes fixed firmly on some distant spot on the horizon.

'It's not obvious at all, and I'd be grateful if you'd explain...Ellie!'

His hand came out, closing over hers, bringing the buggy to such an abrupt halt that it swerved slightly, arcing off the path.

'Explain!'

For a second he thought she was going to refuse to speak, and as she tried to shake off his restraining hand he clamped his fingers more tightly over hers so that she couldn't move.

'Explain,' he repeated in a tone that brooked no argument.

Explain! The word pressed the panic button inside Ellie's

head. She couldn't explain. Not properly. She couldn't tell
him what she had overheard and how it had savaged her
soul. To do so would mean admitting to how much she still
cared for him—how much she *loved* him. Though right now
what she felt for him was closer to hatred than love. It
would mean revealing the hopes and dreams she had allowed herself to feel—the weak, pathetic dreams she should
have known were impossible to come true.

But she had to think of something. There was no way he
was going to let up on this...

'Ellie...'

'You know what I mean.' Desperately she snatched at
inspiration as it struck. 'Kitty Spencer—Macy Renton...'

Her voice was laced with acid as she spat the names into
his face. The names she had listed on that first day in the
cottage. The names of some of the women he had been
linked to in the months since she had fled from his house.

'Oh, them.'

His casual tone was positively the last straw. Would he
have been so carelessly dismissive of her when her time had
come? When he'd tired of her and tossed her aside to move
on to pastures new, fresh excitement?

Well, if that was the case then she was lucky she'd found
out just in time. Lucky she hadn't fallen in so deeply that
she could never climb out.

Only she didn't feel lucky. Instead she felt hopelessly,
totally despondent, as if her world had come to an end and
there was nothing left to live for. And as for falling in too
deep, she'd been there already, right from the start.

'You left a big hole in my life, Ellie. One I tried to fill
any way I could.'

The sapphire eyes held hers as he spoke, almost convincing her with their display of open sincerity.

Almost but not quite. Yesterday she might have been
conned. Yesterday she might have been fool enough to be

drawn into this web of lies just as she had been deceived
by his play of pretending to care for Rosie, not seeing the
machiavellian scheming behind it.

But today she knew better. Today she had had the blind-
fold ripped agonisingly from her eyes. Her vision was clear
and brutally focussed. She knew him for what he was, and
she would never let him dupe her again.

'And I'm supposed to be flattered that it took so many
women to replace me?'

No one replaced you. No one ever could.

The admission almost escaped him, but he bit it back
hastily. The mood she was in, she would never believe it.
Those amber eyes would simply darken with scorn, her neat
chin come up defiantly, the soft curve of her mouth thin to
a hard line.

He knew this mood of old, too. And in the past he had
had a simple technique for bringing her out of it. He would
just grab her, hold her tight—and kiss her senseless. Kiss
both of them senseless. By the time they had come up for
air, they had usually had other things on their minds, things
that had totally distracted them from whatever had caused
the problem in the first place.

But instinct warned him that that was not the way to go
this time. There was something new about Ellie's expression, a touch of vulnerability in her eyes that worried him,
told him to tread carefully.

The problem was that when she looked like this, with her
eyes like molten gold behind the lush, thick lashes, her burnished hair tousled in the wind that blew the green dress
tight against the contours of her body, it was difficult to
think straight. It was near impossible to think of anything
beyond the feel of her in his arms last night. The way those
soft curves had felt to the touch of his hands and his lips,
the sensation of having those long, slender legs entangled
with his.

'That's hardly a very responsible attitude. Haven't you ever heard of AIDS?'

Ah, so now they were getting to the real reason behind her sudden change of mood. The thing that was really bothering her.

'For an intelligent man, you've been indulging in some very stupid behaviour.'

That stung. It stung all the more because he couldn't deny the truth of it. He didn't like the man he'd turned into in the weeks after she'd left. He could only be thankful that it hadn't lasted long and he'd very quickly come to his senses. Luckily before he'd done himself or anyone else any harm.

'Kind of you to be concerned,' he drawled, hiding the truth behind deliberate satire, 'but there's no need. I'm always very careful.'

He would be *careful*. She had thought that nothing else could hurt her any more but this twisted the cruel knife in an already devastated heart. Because now, just when she was too vulnerable to deal with it, another memory came back to haunt her. Last night, except for that first wild, mindless time when passion had driven all thought, all sense of safety or restraint from their thoughts, Morgan had reverted to type. On every other occasion—and there had been many others—he had had enough forethought, enough restraint, to find and use the condoms he had insisted on—to 'protect' them both.

'Careful like you were last night?'

Once again the pallor of her face, the clouded amber eyes were like a reproach, pricking his conscience savagely.

'The first time? I know I made a mistake and I'm sorry about that, Ellie. Believe me, I'm not usually so thoughtless—but if you're worried you needn't be. A while ago I—had a complete health check-up and there was nothing—*nothing* at all to worry about. And as there's been no one since...'

'I'm glad to hear it,' Ellie snapped, sounding exactly the opposite. 'Now if you'll just let me get on...'

Mistake. Thoughtless. If she wanted reinforcement of her reasons not to tell him about Rosie, then there it was in those two revealing words. Needing to express her feelings forcefully, she rammed the pushchair into Morgan's foot, making him jump smartly out of the way.

It hadn't been meant to go this way, Morgan thought wearily as he stood watching her stalk away, her slim back and shoulders stiff with angry rejection. This hadn't been what he'd planned for—what he'd imagined might happen after last night.

It had been in the long, quiet hours of the morning, in the peace of just before dawn when the wildfires of passion had finally burned themselves out and they had both lain still sated and exhausted, too worn out to move, that the idea had first come to him.

Ellie had drifted into a deep sleep almost immediately, but, for all his physical tiredness, his mind had been vividly awake, buzzing with the thrill of knowing that Ellie had come back to him and it could only get better every day from now on.

A faint sound from down the corridor had disturbed him. Rosie stirring and muttering in her sleep. The sort of sound that Ellie, who had so much more experience of these things than he did, didn't even register and probably would have recognised as nothing to worry about if she had. But once he had heard it he had been unable to settle. He couldn't face the prospect of not doing anything in case something was truly wrong.

And so he'd got up as quietly as possible and gone down to the living room where the baby lay in her cot, her small, dark head illuminated by a slanting shaft of moonlight.

She'd been fine, of course. Fast asleep, and making the

stupidest, silliest little baby snore he had ever heard. And it was then that the idea had come to him.

That tiny sound had reached out and coiled round his heart. This kid had got to him in a way he wouldn't have thought possible, sneaking past his defences, finding cracks in the formerly impregnable armour he'd adopted against just such things. And the fact that she was Pete Bedford's child no longer seemed to matter.

He wanted Ellie, and if she came as a package with Rosie, well, that was fine with him. The baby needed a dad. It was as simple as that. For so long he'd lived his life believing that ever being a father was a closed door to him. Now he knew differently. Rosie could almost be the daughter he'd believed he'd never have, and he found that the thought of that actually coming true was one that delighted him.

But there would be no chance of that if he didn't sort things out with Ellie first. Already she was disappearing round the corner and if he didn't hurry she would be in the farm, and, if he knew her, closing the door firmly in his face.

'Ellie!'

Breaking into a jog, he hurried after her, catching her up at the gate into the farm garden.

'Ellie, wait. We have to talk.'

She was still set against him, her eyes hooded, her mouth compressed.

'I don't think so.'

'But we need to talk about the past—what happened between us. The reason why you left.'

'What?'

Desperately she swallowed down the panic that welled up inside her. For a second her eyes dropped to where Rosie sat in the pushchair, mercifully still fast asleep, then flew back up to Morgan's sombre, intent face.

'What is there to say about that?'

'Everything—and the truth this time.'

The world tilted sharply, making her clutch at the handle of the buggy for support.

'I don't know what…'

'I'll make it easy for you, shall I?' Morgan put in when her voice failed her. 'I think I know what you want to say. You see, I know now why you left eighteen months ago—and it really had very little to do with Pete Bedford.'

CHAPTER THIRTEEN

'YOU know why I left?'

Ellie's heart kicked sharply in fear, her fingers tightening over the buggy's handle until the knuckles showed white. She didn't dare look at Rosie, knowing her face would betray her if she did.

'I don't think...' she tried, her voice weak and hoarse, but he held up one hand to silence her.

'I can see now that much of it was my fault. I was wrong to try and impose my wishes on you when we were together. To try and force you into my way of thinking.'

Ellie couldn't believe what she was hearing. Was he saying that if she had tried again, if she had persisted with pushing her side of the argument, he might have given in and changed his mind? Surely it couldn't be that simple.

It wasn't.

'We wanted two very different things from life and our relationship. Obviously you wanted a child—children. I should have known that from the moment I met your parents and brothers. Any fool should have seen that someone who'd grown up in that sort of loving atmosphere would have wanted to create the same sort of family life for themselves as an adult.'

The corners of Morgan's mouth quirked up into a half-smile that tore at Ellie's heart.

'You loved being part of a family; it's a vital element in your make-up. It wasn't like that for me; I didn't see family life that way. But I had no right to deprive you of it. For a while you let me dictate terms, but anyone who wasn't com-

pletely blind could have seen that it wouldn't last. In the
end you couldn't deny your feelings.'

Ellie's swiftly indrawn breath drew a searching glance
from those brilliant blue eyes.

'I'm right, aren't I? Seeing you with Rosie, the way she
completes you, has made it obvious why you couldn't stay
with me. That's why you went to Pete...'

Pete. An icy sense of dread slid down Ellie's spine at the
repetition of the other man's name. Morgan had come so
close to the truth, but it seemed that he had missed it again,
putting a new and disturbing spin on events.

'But what I don't understand,' Morgan went on, his tone
darkening ominously, 'is why the woman who valued family life so much chose to have a child with someone who
clearly wasn't around for the long haul.'

'You—do you really think I'm so shallow that I would
go to Pete just because I wanted a *baby*?'

She could only pray that he thought the quaver in her
voice had been put there by anger. If he saw past the controlled mask she was trying to display, and cut right through
to the anguish that was eating her up inside, she knew it
would destroy her completely

'Not shallow, Ellie.' Morgan's tone was reproving. 'But
you were young—and very impulsive. I think you told me
that you loved me almost the day after we met.'

'Don't remind me,' Ellie growled, gritting her teeth
against the pain of the memory. She had been so wildly,
crazily and—yes—naively in love that she hadn't been able
to wait to tell him. Morgan on the other hand had been
coolly reticent about his feelings, except for his determination not to have children, all the time they'd been together.

'So I'm sure you believed you loved Rosie's father at the
start as well.'

Now could have been the perfect time to tell him, Ellie

thought miserably. In fact, if she hadn't overheard those appalling, revealing words this morning, then Morgan would know by now. He would know the truth about why she had left him—and he would know that *he* was Rosie's father.

'Didn't you?'

'Oh, yes.' Ellie's mouth twisted on the bitterness of the admission. 'Yes, I loved Rosie's father. I thought he was a love for life.'

'We all make mistakes. But Pete wasn't the sort of man you needed. He isn't even here for you—he's marrying someone else.'

'We—we live the way we want,' Ellie blustered desperately.

'Which would be fine if there was no one else involved. But you have a child now. Surely Rosie needs something better than this.'

Ellie felt as if she had found herself in a nightmare world where everything was suddenly turned upside down. Morgan was showing the sort of concern for Rosie that she had prayed he would, but still for those selfish, cruel reasons of his own.

'Don't you think you're being a trifle hypocritical?' she flung at him, goaded beyond endurance by conflicting emotions. 'The man who doesn't want children criticising me for the way I'm bringing up my daughter—isn't that the pot calling the kettle black?'

Now should have been the perfect time to tell her the truth, Morgan thought ruefully. But she was still too hostile, too bitterly guarded to listen. The only thing he could do was to keep on arguing from the position of concern for Rosie. Right now it seemed that that was the one thing that might get through to her.

'My opinions don't come into this. A child needs two parents—a secure home—and I could at least have offered you that. I always did. You never wanted for anything that way.'

'And you think that because you provided for me materially, that was enough? That I wouldn't need anything more? You of all people should know that that's not the case.'

'No.' Morgan's sensual mouth twisted bitterly. 'Obviously there was a great deal missing in our relationship or you'd never have gone. But if you'd conceived my child, then things would have been very different. I would have had a duty to marry you.'

For a brief moment Ellie closed her eyes against the pain. Which would have been harder to bear? Feeling that she had to leave Morgan because he would totally reject his child if he knew of it? Or knowing that he would actually have married her—but only because he'd 'had a duty to'?

'I couldn't force Rosie's father...' there was no way she could say Pete in that context '...to marry me.'

Morgan's response was another of those twisted smiles.

'Not when he's already planning to marry another woman. But perhaps someone else...'

Oh, didn't he ever give up? Ellie thought in despair. Did he really not guess that she'd seen through his scheming, recognised his apparent concern for Rosie's welfare for the act it was? She'd had her face rubbed in the truth and she wasn't likely to forget a lesson so painfully learned in a hurry.

'I'm perfectly capable of coping. I don't need a knight in shining armour rushing to my rescue.'

'No?' Another of those wry, lopsided smiles was almost her undoing. 'I thought that was what every woman wanted.'

'You've been reading too many legends, Morgan. All those stories about Cornwall being the birthplace of King Arthur must have turned your brain. Now, if you don't mind—my grandmother and Henry will be getting frantic wondering where I am.'

They would be doing no such thing. She had rung from the cottage last night to explain where she'd been, and Nan, who was one of the few people who knew the full story of her granddaughter's relationship with Morgan, had been thrilled at the recent developments. That was someone else who was going to be bitterly disillusioned and devastated when she learned the truth.

'I promised I'd be back in time to help Nan pack. She and Henry are going away on a second honeymoon tomorrow, to celebrate the first anniversary of when they met. And I think we've said all there is to say.'

He wasn't getting anywhere at all on this tack, Morgan told himself. Perhaps if he tried a new approach.

'Okay, so you don't want a knight on a charger riding in and taking control—but what about a bit of fun?'

It was the last thing she'd expected. 'Fun?'

'I've seen what your life's like here, and it looks like pretty hard work to me.'

'I don't mind—' Ellie began but Morgan cut across her attempt at protest.

'No social life, no reason to dress up and go out. We used to have a great time, Ellie—the theatre—restaurants.'

He'd hit a chord there; just for a second it showed in her eyes. She had always loved an excuse to put on her finery, make-up, perfume. But just as soon as the flicker of response sparked in the bronze of her eyes he saw how she clamped down hard on the yearning, almost, but not quite, shutting it off.

He pounced on that 'not quite', determined to push home the advantage.

'There's an awards night in a few weeks. The screenplay I did for *The Dark Side of the Moon* has been nominated, so I'm expected to be there. And naturally I can bring a partner.

'Naturally,' Ellie echoed faintly, seeing the path his thoughts were following now and not at all sure she liked it.

'So I thought that you could come up to town—stay for a few days, see the sights, and go to the awards night as my partner. You and Rosie, of course.'

'No!'

If anything was guaranteed to make up her mind for her, it was that carefully planned 'You and Rosie' tacked onto the end.

'Why the hell not, Ellie? What's wrong?'

Everything was wrong. Going up to London meant staying in Morgan's apartment. It meant days of close proximity—*nights*. And she knew just what he would expect from those nights.

'I—I don't have anything to wear.'

In desperation she grabbed at the most unconvincing feminine excuse, expecting, and getting, his scornful laughter in response.

'Oh, Ellie, if that's your only objection—I'll buy you a damn dress! I'll buy you a hundred dresses—anything you want, if you'll just say yes.'

'I don't want you to buy me a dress. I don't want anything from you! I—'

'Good morning, Ellie, my dear!' Ellie recognised the voice that broke in on her as soon as she heard it. 'It is still morning, isn't it—just? And you must be Mr Stafford. We've spoken on the phone, but not actually met in person. My name's Henry—Henry Knightley.'

Ellie was still collecting her scattered thoughts as Morgan responded, taking the hand that the tall, grey-haired man held out to him and shaking it firmly.

'Nice to meet you at last. I understand that you're married to Ellie's grandmother.'

'That's right—we've been together a year on Friday.' Henry beamed proudly.

'And you're planning on a second honeymoon, I believe. Are you going somewhere special?'

'A cruise on the Nile. We leave tomorrow and we'll be away for a fortnight. I wanted to make it a month, but of course Marion wouldn't hear of it. She wanted to make sure she was back in time for the big celebration.'

Through the distraction of her thoughts Ellie suddenly became shockingly aware of just what Henry was talking about, the perilous direction in which the conversation was heading. Panic was like an electrical charge running through her, pushing her into speech before she could think.

'Henry, don't! I mean—Mr Stafford won't be interested in that.'

On the contrary, he was obviously very interested, she realised in despair. Her tone had been too sharp, giving too much away, and now Morgan's blue eyes were turned on her, alert and watchful and touched with a strong dose of suspicion.

'I mean...'

'Oh, I'm sure you're wrong there. Naturally, as one of our guests on the farm, Mr Stafford will be invited to the young madam's birthday party next month.'

Henry was totally oblivious to the dark undercurrents his innocent remarks had sparked off, unaware of the tension between the other two adults. Feeling as if she were watching inevitable disaster rushing towards her with all the speed and unstoppable force of a runaway train, Ellie cursed the promise she had made Nan give her. If Henry had known of Morgan's connection with Rosie, he would never have blundered in like this.

'He...'

'Young madam?'

Morgan's echoing of Henry's words clashed with her own weak attempt at speech, freezing the words on her tongue. His eyes were ice-cold now, pinning her to the spot, his searching gaze taking in her white, pallid cheeks, the wide, overbright eyes with the speculative assessment that he might turn on a particularly nasty specimen he had to view under a microscope.

'But your birthday's in March...'

Despairingly Ellie thought that she could almost hear his mind working, counting out the number of months since she had left him, adding the age she had told him Rosie was—changing it.

'Not Ellie's birthday!' Henry laughed, unknowingly banging the last nail into the coffin of Ellie's hopes of avoiding the confrontation she could see looming. 'It's Rosie we're having the party for—after all, a first birthday is something really special.'

'Henry, no!'

But it was already too late.

'Rosie.' Morgan's use of the name was low and savage. 'She's eleven months old, not eight.'

And eleven months old meant that the baby was not Pete Bedford's child. She had nothing to do with the other man, but everything to do with why Ellie had left him.

'Yes, there's someone else,' she had said. 'Someone very, very special. Someone I can't bear to be without.'

And like a damn fool he had jumped to the conclusion that she meant another man. When instead she had meant this child—this perfect, delightful child—and she was *his*. The child he'd never let himself dream of. The child he'd always told himself he could never have. She'd been in the world almost a year and he had never known.

'Morgan...' Ellie tried to reach him, though it was obvious that wherever his mind was it was locked away from her. His face was white with fury, blue eyes ablaze, skin stretched tight across the broad cheekbones.

'You let me think…'

Where the hell was that switch in his mind, the one he'd always been able to employ in the past? Somewhere along the line he had lost the knack of turning off unwanted feelings, of refusing to let them in. This one wouldn't be turned away, and it was almost more than he could bear.

He had a daughter. Rosie was *his* child. And Ellie had known that even before she'd left him eighteen months ago. She had known and she had led him to believe…

'You lied to me!' It was the roar of a wounded lion because the lie was the worst betrayal of all. 'You let me think the kid…'

He couldn't say her name out loud. Couldn't say 'Rosie'. Couldn't say what he most wanted to say—You let me think that *my daughter* was Pete's!

'Morgan, please…'

But something about the atmosphere, the sound of the barely controlled fury in her father's voice, had reached the baby, bringing her out of her doze. Stirring slightly, she opened sleepy blue eyes, lifted her dark head.

His eyes. His colouring. How had he not known? He should have known!

Ellie made a move towards him, her hand outstretched, begging him to understand.

And it was too much. Whirling on his heel, he knew he had to get out of here before he did something *really* stupid. He heard her call after him, just once more, her voice high and tight, and he ignored it, kept on going without a single backward glance.

Watching him go, Ellie knew with a terrible sense of despair that it was just as she'd always imagined his reaction would be when Morgan discovered the truth about Rosie. He had behaved exactly as she had feared he would, walking away from her and the baby without a single hesitation. Only this time, it was much, much worse, because now the scene wasn't being played out in her imagination.

This time it was appallingly, terrifyingly real.

CHAPTER FOURTEEN

THE sound of the doorbell ringing on and on was positively the last straw as far as Ellie was concerned. After a sleepless night, the arrival of the day had brought no let-up in the tension that had gripped her, and the rain that had started to fall the previous evening continued to pour down outside, its endless pattering preying on her nerves until she was ready to scream.

And to make matters worse, Rosie was clearly unwell. The baby had slept only fitfully, waking miserable and fussy, and it had been all Ellie could do to persuade her grandmother and Henry to go on their trip as they had planned.

'It's probably just a cold—she was definitely snuffly in the night—but that's all,' she had assured them. 'And you've been planning this for weeks—you have to go.'

The taxi had barely pulled away from the farmhouse before Rosie had been sick all over her cot. And it was as Ellie was changing the sheets and trying to pacify the fractious baby that the imperious summons of the doorbell sounded once more, pushing her over the edge into unreasoning anger.

'Yes?' she demanded furiously as she yanked open the door. Her mood changed abruptly, all annoyance escaping in a rush, leaving her limp as a pricked balloon as she realised who stood outside.

Morgan looked tired and decidedly the worse for wear, his strong jawline darkened by a heavy stubble, and the sapphire eyes dull and clouded, the shadows underneath them seeming to indicate that he had had no more sleep

159

than she had managed herself. His shoulders were hunched
against the rain and his dark hair was soaked through, plas-
tered against the strong bones of his skull by the heavy
downpour.

'I want to see Rosie,' he announced baldly, his tone flat
and lifeless.

'It's not the best time,' Ellie admitted with weary honesty. 'I...'

She never completed the sentence, her words interrupted
by a shriek from upstairs that had her turning and dashing
back up to the baby's bedroom, leaving the front door wide
open. It was as she lifted Rosie from her cot and cuddled
her close, crooning soothingly, that she realised that Morgan
was right behind her.

'Ellie, she's burning up.'

The blue eyes had taken in the situation in a glance,
Rosie's flushed face telling its own story, one that Morgan
swiftly confirmed by a gentle hand laid on the little girl's
forehead.

'Has she been like this all night?'

'She's been miserable—but this just started this morning.
She's been sick...'

There was no strength in her voice and it wobbled desperately as she laid her head against the baby's burning
cheek. It seemed that in the few moments she had been
downstairs Rosie's temperature had shot up by another couple of degrees.

'Have you phoned the doctor?'

'I was just going to when you...'

But she was speaking to empty air; Morgan was already
halfway down the stairs. A few seconds later she heard his
voice, crisp and incisive, as he explained the situation to
someone on the telephone.

'He'll be here straight away,' he told her as he came back
into the bedroom.

'You spoke to Dr Renfrew himself?' Ellie was frankly astonished, knowing how hard it was to convince the doctor's formidable receptionist that he should be troubled for anything other than a major disaster.

'Once I'd got past the dragon.' Morgan's dry humour did nothing to conceal the ruthless determination that left Ellie in no doubt as to why his opponent had capitulated so easily. 'Here, let me take her—she must be heavy.'

'I've managed before!' Ellie snapped, struggling for control over the emotions that had been swinging up and down in the most disturbing way since she had realised who was at the door. 'I've had to!'

'Then at least sit down!'

He almost pushed her down into the chair, holding her until she settled Rosie in her lap before moving away to lean against the wall, eyes hooded, his face unreadable.

'Are you on your own? Have Henry and Marion gone?'

'I told them to leave—though Nan didn't want to. She's been looking forward to this trip for ages!'

'You always were too damn independent for your own good,' Morgan growled. 'But what would you have done if you'd needed a prescription picking up—or transport...?'

'I'd have managed. Just who do you think you are, lecturing me on how to look after my own daughter?'

'You tell me I'm her father,' Morgan said with deadly quiet.

'Only by a biological accident!'

Ellie no longer cared what she flung at him, wanting only to hurt as he had hurt her so desperately by walking away yesterday.

'You're her *sire*, true—but real fathers do more than just help create a child. They're there when they're needed, when—'

'Did you give me a chance?' His tone was savage, tearing into her tirade like the slash of a knife. 'Did you even condescend to let me know that you were pregnant—or that Rosie had been born?'

Shocked into silence by the force of his attack, Ellie could only stare in confusion and disbelief.

'Are you telling me…?' she began, her thoughts hazing painfully. 'I thought…I was afraid…'

What she had feared was devastatingly obvious. It was etched into her face, darkening her eyes and making them brim with tears. The realisation of just what she meant was like a blow to Morgan's heart, making it feel as if it had actually stopped beating for a long, agonising moment.

'Dear God, Ellie,' he croaked rawly. 'You don't—you can't believe I'd have asked *that* of you.'

Ellie could read nothing but truth in the darkness of his eyes. His gaze reflected her own private horror at the thought of her getting rid of her baby, the total rejection of any such thing.

So had she been so completely wrong to even suspect him?

The taut silence that enclosed them was shattered abruptly by the sound of a car drawing to a halt outside, the slam of its door intruding into the enclosed, intent world they had created.

'The doctor…' Ellie began shakily, but Morgan refused to be distracted.

'Will you give me that chance now, Ellie?' he asked, dark eyes burning into hers. 'Will you?'

Ellie's heart clenched painfully inside her chest as she struggled to find a way to answer him. Had she been wrong to distrust him from the start? But even if she had, how could she forget his reaction yesterday when he had just turned his back and walked away?

But then she looked into Morgan's face and in that second every other thought was wiped from her mind. She was only aware of the open need, the yearning hunger that was stamped onto his stunning features as he looked down at the baby in her arms. Her heart kicked again, making her catch her breath sharply as she admitted to herself that there was only one way she could possibly answer his urgent question.

'Yes,' she said softly, her voice trembling on the single syllable, and she felt the blazing look he turned on her sear her skin from head to toe.

'Thank you,' he said with hoarse-voiced fervour, the rawness of his emotion twisting in her nerves. 'I promise you, you won't regret that.'

But a second later it was as if a mask had been pulled on over his handsome face and he was once more calm, composed and totally in control, only a faintly bruised look about his eyes betraying the storm of emotion that had burned in him.

'I'll let the doctor in,' he said and was gone before Ellie could say another word.

Later, Ellie was to remember that time as a small oasis of calm before the nightmare really took a hold. From the moment of the doctor's arrival, life seemed to speed up until it was running like a film played too fast and nothing in it truly registered except for the fact that Rosie was very ill indeed.

They had to get her to hospital quickly, the doctor said. And then he used the word Ellie had dreaded right from the start. Meningitis. He feared that the baby had meningitis.

At that point Ellie's brain shut down and she simply went through things on autopilot. She was vaguely aware of talk of an ambulance, of Morgan's insistence that they didn't have time, and then being bundled into the car, sitting in a state of shock while he drove like a maniac through the winding country roads heading for town.

The hardest part was handing over the little girl, even to the attentive doctors and nurses, and knowing that there was nothing she could do but sit—and wait. Eventually they were let into the room where Rosie now lay, a tiny, helpless figure, limp as a rag doll amongst an array of tubes and dials that were to monitor her progress, provide the medication she needed.

Seeing her like that, looking so lost and alone, Ellie felt her legs almost go from under her. But Morgan was there beside her in a second, gathering her up into his arms and holding her, until she felt something of his strength flood back into her and the moment of weakness left her.

'Oh, Morgan!' she whispered. 'My baby…'

'I know…'

His voice was as raw as hers and looking into his face she saw how pale he was, the painful tightness of every muscle in his jaw, the glittering sheen of tears in his eyes.

'Oh, Morgan…' she said again, and for a long, long moment they simply held each other, Morgan's head against hers, his cheek resting on the softness of her hair, not saying another word, simply sharing the pain, the fear, the disbelief and the desperation.

Eventually Morgan stirred and lifted his head.

'Come and sit down,' he said gently. 'You're going to need your strength. It looks as if it's going to be a long, long day.'

It was the longest day Ellie had ever known, and it was followed by an even longer night. But time seemed to have no meaning, the hours blurring into each other, marked only by the constant visits of the doctors or nurses, the endless offers of cups of tea that she always agreed to because they were so well meant, but could never swallow when they came.

And all the time Morgan was there, silent, tense, withdrawn, but always supportive. Always there if she looked for him, always ready to do anything she asked of him, or simply stay quiet if that was what she needed. Which was what she needed most of the time.

The walls of the little room were decorated with a bright frieze of Winnie the Pooh and his friends that wound its way around behind the bed that was far too big for its occupant, occasionally hidden by the banks of machines, the antibiotic drip.

'If—if anything happens...' Ellie managed, her voice cracking painfully. '...I'm never going to be able to look at a Pooh book ever again, as long as I live.'

'Ellie, don't!'

He reached for her free hand, the one not laced with Rosie's small, limp fingers, and held it tight.

'Nothing's going to happen. I can't have found my daughter only to lose her again like this—it can't happen. It won't!'

Ellie managed a wobbly smile in response to his vehemence.

'Can—can you promise that?'

The grip on her hand tightened convulsively.

'No, I can't promise, but if I know anything about Rosie she'll be a fighter like her mother.'

'She's very like her father too,' Ellie offered gently. 'Stubborn as hell when challenged.'

'Really?' The lightening of his expression, the faint smile, revealed how much her words had meant. 'Well, in that case, she won't lose. She'll beat this thing, Ellie—she has to.'

It was a while later that Ellie realised that Morgan still held her hand, hard fingers curled tightly round hers. And after that it seemed only natural to leave it there, warm and comforting when she so desperately needed comfort.

Hours passed. Hours in which each second ticked by with agonising slowness, hours where everything remained the same. Which was a good sign, the doctors said. Rosie was holding her own.

Holding her own. It was so little to cling to in the darkness of the night when everyone was asleep except for them. Morgan's eyes ached from watching the little girl's face for some change; he knew he should be exhausted but felt no fatigue. In fact he felt nothing, only a dreadful, deadening numbness that seemed to have reached right through to his soul. Every instinct he possessed cried out to him to act, to help, to *do something*, but the worst thing was knowing there was nothing he could do.

Except wait.

'Will you tell me about Rosie?' he asked and watched Ellie's downbent head lift, her dull, shadowed eyes looking into his.

'What would you like to know?'

'Anything—right from the start. Was it a difficult pregnancy?'

'I've nothing to compare it to. Oh, I had some morning sickness which was foul, and I got tired.'

She choked back the urge to tell him how low she had felt, the way that her days and nights—particularly the nights—had been so empty without him.

'And of course she decided to be born at the ungodly hour of three in the morning.'

'What sort of a baby was she?'

'Perfect. Most of the time I hardly knew she was there. She slept when I wanted her to, soon fell into a manageable routine. I was so lucky really. She always loved being taken places in her pram, and being sung to. But really bathtime was the highlight of the day—she adored splashing around and we always ended up with bubbles everywhere.'

Suddenly she couldn't meet his eyes, knowing just what had put the shadows in them. If the worst happened, she would at least have her memories of Rosie, however brief. Morgan wouldn't have even that.

'Did you do it deliberately?'

The sudden question startled her.

'Do what?'

'Conceive Rosie. Did you...?'

'Oh, no!' Fearful that he might think she had used him or set out to force his hand, she hurriedly reassured him. 'It wasn't like that at all. It was that time I had that dreadful migraine. I forgot to take my pill. By the time I remembered it was too late. When I realised I was pregnant, I just panicked. I knew you were so dead set against the idea of children—'

'I'd *told myself* I didn't want children,' Morgan interjected harshly. 'In fact I told myself that so many times that in the end I actually came to believe it.'

Ellie stared at him in bewilderment and confusion, unable to understand what he was telling her.

'What does that mean, Morgan? What do you mean you told yourself?'

The sapphire gaze slid away from hers to stare fixedly at a point on the far wall, though Ellie was convinced that he wasn't actually seeing anything.

'Later,' he muttered roughly. 'You have enough on your plate right now.'

'No. Tell me about it. I want to know.'

She still thought that he might refuse. That he would shut her out and say nothing at all. But at last he sighed and rubbed the back of his hand across his eyes in a gesture of weary resignation.

'It was something I learned when I was twelve.' He spoke in a flat, emotionless monotone that drove a bitter cold into Ellie's bones simply to hear it. 'Just as soon as I started showing interest in girls, my mother decided it was time I knew the truth about my father, and the real reason he got so drunk that night.'

He didn't say which night; he didn't have to. Ellie knew exactly what he meant—the night his father had driven his car in front of a train.

'He'd been to the doctor's that morning, for the results of some tests. Those tests confirmed what he'd already suspected—have you ever heard of Huntington's disease?'

'A—a little,' Ellie stammered, taken aback by the abrupt change of subject. 'It's a brain disorder, isn't it? One that starts by causing awkward, jerky movements and eventually leads to dementia?'

Morgan nodded slowly, his expression grim.

'It's also a killer—and it's genetic.'

'Genetic…' Ellie's mind reeled in horror as she realised what he was trying to tell her. 'Do you mean that your father had this awful disease?'

She read his answer in his eyes before he actually nodded a reluctant confirmation.

'And you…?'

'I had a fifty-fifty chance of getting it too. And if I had it, or if I was a carrier, then any child of mine ran that risk too.'

'Oh, my God! Are you telling me that Rosie—'

'No!'

Morgan caught hold of the hands that she had raised to cover her mouth, as if to hold back the dreadful truth, and squeezed them hard.

'No, Ellie—Rosie's safe—though for a long time I believed that any child of mine would inherit the family curse.'

'Are you sure?'

'Positive. Do you remember I told you I'd had some major medical check-ups? Well, I had the tests—and more—

done, and they could be one-hundred-per-cent certain that I was clear.'

His mouth twisted suddenly.

'So much so that it's likely the poor guy wasn't even my father. Probably my mother didn't even know exactly who had fathered me.'

'But you always believed...' Ellie was struggling with the deeper implications of what he was telling her. 'Morgan, when we were together...'

His silence gave her all the answer she needed.

'So that's why you said you never wanted children?'

'I knew I couldn't risk passing on something like that. So I told myself that kids didn't matter, that I didn't ever want them anyway.'

His laughter was harsh, terrifying, without any trace of humour in it at all, making Ellie flinch back in her chair in distress.

'That's the sort of thing that's easy to convince yourself of when you're just in your twenties, and over the years it became so much a part of my way of thinking that I felt as if it had always been there—that it was what I truly felt.'

'But why didn't you take the test?'

'In the beginning it didn't matter. There was no one else it was ever going to affect, I vowed I'd make sure of that. The question of children didn't crop up because I hadn't found anyone I'd want to be their mother. I'd never met any woman with whom I wanted to spend the rest of my life. And—hell, I'll admit it—I was a damn coward. I didn't want to know. If it was what was ahead of me, I'd face it when I had to, not before.'

'I wouldn't call that cowardice.' Ellie's voice was soft. 'It was a decision I'm not sure I could make.'

'But it was also a decision that deprived me of seeing my baby born—that meant I missed the first year of her life.'

And Ellie couldn't doubt just what that had meant to him.

'Morgan...' she began hesitantly. 'When this is over...you and Rosie...'

But Morgan wasn't listening. Instead his head had turned, his eyes were fixed on the man who stood in the doorway—the consultant who was in charge of Rosie's case.

'Mr and Mrs Thornton...'

It was a natural mistake to make, Ellie supposed. In the first dreadful minutes of their arrival at the hospital she had registered her baby as Rosie Thornton without thinking. It was only when she had seen Morgan's face whiten that she had realised what message it must have given him.

But then Morgan said, 'Yes?' in a tone that sent shivers down her spine and she suddenly realised just what might be happening.

'Morgan...'

Automatically her hand went out to him as she got shakily to her feet, but he was already there, powerful arms encircling her, holding her tight.

Through the buzzing in her head she heard what was said but couldn't take it in, even though the doctor repeated it at Morgan's insistence.

'What?' she asked fearfully. 'What are you telling me?'

'It's *not* meningitis, angel.'

Somehow Morgan's voice got through where no one else's could.

'Rosie doesn't have meningitis. It's some form of really vicious virus, but it's not *that*. She's going to be okay.'

'She's going to be...'

It didn't seem possible. But the doctor was nodding and smiling and the grin on Morgan's shadowed face told its own story.

'Your daughter's still a very sick little girl, but we're positive she's going to make a full recovery.'

'Rosie's going to get better.' Ellie choked and then the effect of the best news ever hit home and did what none of

the horrors of the previous day had been able to do—it
reduced her to tears.

Not just tears but racking, heaving great sobs that shook
her slim body with a terrible violence. Her legs felt weak
beneath her and she knew that without Morgan's solid support she would collapse in a pathetic heap on the floor.
Instead she buried her head against the strength of his chest
and gave in to the force of her emotions.

And Morgan simply folded his arms round her and held
her tight for as long as she needed.

CHAPTER FIFTEEN

'I'M SORRY, Miss Thornton.'

The housekeeper Morgan employed in his London apartment and who had been left in charge of Rosie for the evening looked stunned and embarrassed.

'She was fast asleep when I looked in only five minutes ago. I don't have the faintest idea what woke her.'

'It's all right, Mrs Cole,' Ellie hastened to reassure the older woman. 'It was probably the sound of us arriving that disturbed Rosie.'

More likely the sound of Morgan's voice, she thought with an inward smile. The adoration that the baby had developed for her new-found father, which had begun really from the day they had met, was so strong that Rosie seemed to sense when Morgan was around, and quite simply refused to let him out of her sight.

And the devotion was mutual, she added wryly as Mrs Cole left in the taxi that had been provided for her, and Morgan, who had headed upstairs at the first hint of the baby's cry, now reappeared. Rosie was perched blissfully in the crook of his arm, her head against his shoulder, beaming her delight up into his face.

'Morgan, you were supposed to settle her back to sleep—not bring her down again!'

She tried to make her words sound like a reproof but failed miserably when faced with the luminous glow in both pairs of blue eyes, the smile that softened Morgan's hard features as he hugged his daughter close. Still dressed in the elegant black and white of formal evening wear, he had a heart-stoppingly sensual appeal that dried her mouth just to see it. The superbly tailored lines of the jacket hugged his powerful chest and broad straight shoulders like a glove and the fine material of the trousers enhanced the forceful impact of a narrow waist and long, long legs.

'She's not sick any more. You don't need to fuss over her quite so much.'

'I'm not fussing,' he protested. 'I just wanted her to be part of this special evening. Look, monster...'

With his free hand he caught up the trophy he had received earlier that evening—the award for the best screenplay—and held it out to the little girl.

'Look what Daddy won tonight.'

'Dada, dodo di!' Rosie shrieked, reaching out to try and grab the golden quill pen that formed part of the trophy.

'She says she has the cleverest daddy in all the world,' Morgan translated proudly.

'Not so clever when it comes to making sure that other people get a good night's sleep,' Ellie retorted tartly. 'I trust you are going to be the one who will stay up with her until she condescends to doze off again at some point?'

She was grateful for the excuse to hide her true feelings under the disguise of indignation. Just to see Morgan and Rosie together seemed to tear her heart in all directions with the conflict between some very difficult feelings.

Ever since the baby had come round in the hospital, and with every day that had passed after that, the delight of seeing Rosie grow stronger had been combined with the bitter-sweet experience of watching the love affair between father and daughter develop like a raging forest fire that had swept through her life, changing it for ever.

She would have to have been all sorts of a fool not to be overjoyed by the happiness the two of them had found together, but at the same time she couldn't help feeling painfully left out, very much on the sidelines. Morgan adored his daughter and wanted to be a major part of her life, that much was obvious. But in the couple of weeks since Rosie's illness he had never said a single word about what his plans were for the future.

He might want the baby, but did he want her mother as well? Because in that question were the seeds of a possible lifetime of pain for Ellie herself.

'I'd never met any woman with whom I wanted to spend the rest of my life.' The words Morgan had spoken on the first night of Rosie's illness came back to haunt her. *Never*. That put her exactly in her place—and that place wasn't in Morgan's future.

'Did I tell you how beautiful you're looking tonight?'

Morgan's sudden, soft-voiced question startled Ellie, her eyes flying to his face in surprise.

He was looking at her over the baby's dark head and in his eyes was an expression she hadn't seen for days. Not since the moment when he had first discovered the truth about Rosie.

'Morgan…' she croaked, her throat drying as if in the molten heat of his gaze as she stroked her hands down the tight skirt of her dress in a gesture of flustered embarrassment.

The dress, in a burnished bronze silk *dévoré* velvet, had been one that Morgan had insisted on buying for her. Tight-fitting and sleeveless, supported by the finest of shoestring straps, it clung lovingly to every curve of her body, making her supremely aware of her femininity, especially now with Morgan's darkened eyes resting on her.

'You look wonderful,' he said, his voice as softly husky as hers. 'I was so proud to have you by my side tonight.'

'And I was proud to be there.'

The truth was that she was still reeling slightly with the speed at which her life had changed. When Morgan had first mentioned the awards night, she had never imagined that by the time it came around she would actually be here, with Rosie, and that Morgan would have claimed the little girl as his daughter quite as definitely as he had done.

If only he would claim her as well. The thought slid unwanted but irresistibly into her mind. The hunger to have him take her in his arms, hold her, kiss her was like a storm in her blood so that she was sure that, standing so close, he must hear how her heart was racing, see the uneven speed of her breathing.

But the truth was that as Morgan had grown closer to Rosie he seemed to have become more and more distant from Ellie herself. Even here, in his London apartment, he had carefully arranged for separate bedrooms for them all, and Ellie would have to be completely blind not to see the message he wanted to get across.

'Morgan...' she said again, but something had broken the spell and, seeing his instant withdrawal, she cursed herself for speaking at all. It was as if steel doors had slammed shut behind the blue eyes, locking her out so forcefully that her head reeled as if from an actual physical blow.

'You're right,' he said with an abrupt change of tone. 'Rosie should be in bed. Come on, monster. Little girls who are only just out of hospital need their sleep. Why don't you make some coffee?' he tossed over his shoulder as he headed back up the stairs. 'I'm sure we could both do with one.'

Coffee might warm her body, Ellie reflected as she headed drearily for the kitchen, but she doubted if it would do anything to melt the freezing ice that seemed to have enclosed her heart.

In the hospital it had been so different. There, while Rosie had still been so ill, when the doctors had still been concerned about her temperature, she and Morgan had worked as a team. No man could have cared more, done more for his daughter. He hadn't flinched from any of the less pleasant aspects of caring for a child, particularly a sick one, and he had shared her vigil in the little girl's room with an almost telepathic understanding.

There was one particular occasion she knew would live in her memory for ever. After three terribly disturbed nights she had finally succumbed to exhaustion, falling asleep in her chair by the bed, and had woken to find that Morgan had picked her up and carried her to the small private room he had arranged for the hospital to provide. A room that, she later discovered, Morgan had paid for, as he had paid for everything else that Rosie had needed.

Discovering to her shock that it was almost ten, she had hurried to Rosie's bedroom to discover that Morgan was still in his chair by his daughter's bed but that he too had fallen asleep where he was. But one arm still lay between the bars of Rosie's cot, her hand in his, the baby's tiny fingers totally enclosed by the man's large, powerful ones.

'It's almost like old times, finding you in my kitchen.' Morgan's voice came from behind, startling her so that the teaspoon she had been using clattered onto the workshop.

'Not quite…' she began but as she turned to face him the words shrivelled in her throat.

That look was back in his eyes again. The dark-eyed, sultry, seductive look that made her skin tingle, her blood heat where it touched.

'So you never actually stayed here.' Morgan shrugged off the comment as the irrelevancy it was. 'It's still good to have you in my home after all this time.'

'We—had some happy times.' Her voice went up and down embarrassingly.

'But not happy enough, hmm?'

He strolled into the room, coming dangerously close. Far too close for her peace of mind. The height and width of his body seemed to fill the small room and the scent of his aftershave tormented nostrils that, like all the rest of her body, were abnormally sensitive to his presence beside her.

'So what was it that kept us together for so long?'

It was that tone of voice again. The husky, seductive purr that told her exactly what was on his mind. It was there in the tension in Morgan's face too, in the way that his skin was drawn tight over the hard bones, the sensual fire in his eyes, the pressure of his hands as he reached out and caught her by the shoulders, turning her to face him fully.

And the same thing was on her mind too. Her heart was thudding, her body trembling with hunger. She knew the instant that Morgan read her thoughts on her face, saw it in the lazily triumphant smile that curled his lips.

'Oh, yes,' he said, his voice thick and rough. 'Yes, angel, that's what kept you with me.'

One hand slid up over the delicate skin of her throat and under her chin, lifting her mouth to his. At the first touch of his lips on hers the searing physical need that she had been struggling to tamp down flared into crackling life like a well-laid bonfire bursting into flame at just the touch of a match.

'This is what was always right between us,' Morgan murmured against her mouth. 'This was never complicated, never went sour. Even on the night before you left.'

'Please!'

Ellie closed her eyes against the pain that flashed through her. Believing that she had had no choice but to leave him, she had put off the terrible moment of telling him for one last time. And that night when she and Morgan had made love the painful secret she had been forced to keep hidden seemed to have sharpened her responses, sensitised every nerve so that the passion between them had never been so overwhelming, every pleasure sharp as a pain.

And she felt the same way now, hearing his whisper against her ear, his breath warm and soft as his voice.

'Ellie, I want you. I need you. Just one more time.'

She knew she was not strong enough to deny both him

and herself because the hungry clamour in her body told her with brutal clarity that this was what she wanted too.

As he gathered her close and pressed hard, hungry kisses on her mouth Ellie knew that she didn't care—couldn't care what name he gave to this. She called it love. He labelled it wanting—need—but what did it matter in the end? It all came down to the same feelings, and those feelings were what she longed for right now.

'Ellie?'

She didn't care if the softness of her name hid a lie. She only knew that what she wanted was to have him hold her, kiss her, warm her aching heart. But most of all she wanted him to stop her thinking for a while.

'Yes,' she whispered, her voice low and shaken. 'Oh, Morgan—yes!'

And then it was exactly as she had wished, with all thought suspended and sheer sensation taking over. He led her to the settee and kissed her until she was dizzy, her body stirring to life under his caresses. She barely noticed the ease with which the velvet dress was stripped from her body, the careless speed with which he discarded his own elegant clothes. What she wanted was the total union, the most complete form of communication that was possible between a man and a woman.

Every touch, every caress was like a voyage of rediscovery. It was like returning to some wonderfully beautiful place she had once known but in the past had only seen with imperfect vision, as though through clouded glass. Now it was so clear and bright that it hurt her eyes and her heart to look at it.

'Morgan!' His name was a sob of delight on her lips as his mouth fastened on her nipple, tugging softly. 'Oh, Morgan, Morgan, Morgan!'

She was burning up as if in a fever as he thrust into her, everything seeming to be etched so sharply onto her brain that she knew this memory would never fade, no matter how much time passed. She saw the male beauty of Morgan's body, the width of chest that narrowed down to a lean waist and hips, the ebony silk of his hair as it slid under her fingertips. The scent of his skin filled her nostrils and she was drowning in sensation, adrift on a heated sea of pleasure in which every sense had been reborn, coming newly, exquisitely awake.

But there was one place that she couldn't look; one part of him that she was afraid to see. She could not meet his sapphire gaze because she feared that if she did then she would see only the need, the passion that he had spoken of, and nothing of the love that she so desperately needed.

His desire she could have no doubt of. Every touch, every kiss, every movement of his body communicated that so eloquently. But that vital element, the one thing that would change this passion from simply an act of lust into an act of love, was something she feared he was incapable of feeling.

And so she kept her eyes lowered or closed, finding that, as if she were blind, the darkness heightened every sensation, sending delight spiralling through her in waves of fire. That heat built up and up into an intolerable tension that, just as she thought she could stand no more, suddenly exploded into a moment of white-hot ecstasy so that she felt as if her body and mind had shattered into a million tiny pieces, each one as diamond-bright as the most brilliant, beautiful star.

For a long time she lay limp and unthinking, her heart still racing, her mind empty and clear like a window washed clean by a violent rainstorm. But Morgan's sudden movement, the violent way that he jerked away from her, broke into her dream world, shattering it brutally.

'Morgan?'

Stunned by the abrupt change in mood, she sat up slowly,

watching in disbelief as he snatched up his trousers and pulled them on, tossing her dress towards her with rough impatience.

'Put it on,' he ordered.

She didn't dare to protest, his expression frightened her too much. She didn't know what had changed but the blue eyes that had earlier glowed like polished gems now seemed to have turned to sapphire ice.

Morgan barely gave her time to pull on the dress and smooth it down before he rounded on her once again.

'Ellie, this can't go on. You have to marry me.'

'Have to?' she echoed incredulously. '*Have to!* But why?'

'Isn't it obvious? Because of Rosie. I want to give her a home. Give her my name.'

Of course. She should have known that this was coming. In her mind she was once again back in the farmhouse garden, hearing Morgan say, 'If you'd conceived my child...I would have had a duty to marry you.'

'Rosie already has a name!' In her pain she flung it at him with all the defiance she could muster. 'A perfectly adequate one. She doesn't need another.'

Morgan's glare was dark as a thundercloud and she shrank back against the settee, fearful of the lightning bolt of fury that must inevitably accompany it.

'Yes, she has a name—but Rosie *Thornton's* not her real name. Her real name is Rosie *Stafford*. Do you know what it did to me in that hospital to know that I paid for all her care, everything she needed, but she didn't have *her father's* name?'

'And you think that paying for things is what makes you a father?'

She knew the question wasn't fair, knew she was being deliberately provocative, but her pain was such that she had to lash out in some way. It was either that or run, mortally wounded, from the room, and never, ever face him again.

'No, I do not think that paying for things makes me a father,' Morgan declared savagely, wild flames of fury flaring in his eyes. 'What made me a father was the total despair I knew when I couldn't help my child. The feeling that I would willingly die in her place if it meant that she would recover. Then I knew that I was truly Rosie's father.'

The simple eloquence of the declaration brought the sting of tears to Ellie's eyes. She had been totally unjust and she knew it.

'I'm sorry,' she whispered. 'I should never have said that. Please forgive me. You're a great father, especially since you were pushed headlong into the reality of it all by Rosie's illness—a real baptism of fire.'

'It was probably best that way. I didn't have time to think. I was scared stiff, but I had no choice. There was this tiny scrap of humanity totally dependent on me.'

'And you coped brilliantly.' She owed him that at the very least.

'She's *my daughter* Ellie.' The lovingly possessive note on the word said all that needed to be said. 'She's my own private miracle, the one I thought I'd never see. So you see why I want Rosie to have my name—and you'll marry me?'

'Marry you? Oh, no.'

She couldn't marry a man who didn't love her. A man who had only proposed out of a sense of duty and because he wanted his daughter to have his name.

'Don't worry, Morgan.' Ellie struggled to hide her own sadness. 'I won't be difficult about things. You can have access to her whenever you want.'

Morgan felt as if he had been punched hard in the stomach. Did she really think that would be enough? How the hell was he supposed to cope with seeing her so often, because of Rosie and only because of Rosie, nothing else?

'*Access!*' he exploded. 'I don't want access! That's not how I want things to be at all. It's not good enough. Rosie's mine. She needs a father—a real father like you said. I'll not have her thinking that some other man...'

'Other man? What other man?'

Unable to sit still any longer, Ellie pushed herself to her feet so that she could face him directly, look into his eyes.

'Morgan, there is no other man. You know there never was.'

'And never will be! I'll not let someone else take my place...'

Ellie felt her blood chill in fearful apprehension at the thought of where all this might be leading.

'What exactly do you want?'

'Isn't it obvious?' he flung at her, blue eyes blazing, shoulders tight with aggression. 'I want the family I never had as a child. I don't want to be some part-time father.'

The cold sensation in Ellie's veins had reached her heart, freezing it cruelly.

'I won't let you do that. I'll never let Rosie go! I'm her mother and a mother's place is—'

'With her child, of course. I'm not asking you to give her up. I expect you to come as well.'

The ice hadn't numbed her heart at all, Ellie realised. Instead she felt every agonising moment as it tore slowly in two. Morgan was still set on carrying out what he believed to be his duty.

'You'd do that to get Rosie?'

Of course he'd do it. It would be the only thing that would give his life a meaning, make his future worthwhile. And he'd thought there was enough between them to have a hope of making it work. But Ellie had pretty soon disillusioned him on that score.

'To get *you and Rosie*. How could you imagine that I'd

ever consider separating you? Ellie, I know there's nothing between us but sex...'

Oh, he was nothing if not blunt, Ellie thought wretchedly, wrapping her arms tight around herself to protect herself from the pain. But then Morgan's next words turned her world upside down and inside out.

'On your part, at least.'

'On my... When did I say...?'

'Oh, come on Ellie!' Morgan dismissed her half-formed protest roughly. 'You didn't have to *say* anything. When I made love to you, you couldn't even look me in the face!'

'Because I was scared!'

It was just a thin thread of sound but Morgan caught it and stilled suddenly, blue eyes narrowing sharply.

'What did you say?'

'Because I was scared.'

Ellie flung it at him this time. She might as well tell him the truth; she couldn't hurt any more than she already did.

'I couldn't look at you because I knew I'd never be able to bear it if I saw in your face that you didn't love me.'

'*Love.*' Morgan pounced on the word. 'And did that matter to you?'

'Of course it did!' Ellie was beyond caring what she revealed now. 'I couldn't let you make love to me without some love somewhere.'

'But you thought that *I* didn't love you. So that love was on *your* side? Ellie...' Morgan prompted when she couldn't respond.

She couldn't meet his intent gaze. 'If you must know—yes!'

'Oh, thank God!'

The fervent exclamation brought her lowered lids up in a rush, her thoughts spinning as she saw the luminous glow that lit his eyes from within.

'I thought I'd never hear you say that.'

'But you... Morgan, you called me the worst mistake of your life, one you'd regret as long as you lived!'

'No.'

Suddenly he came to her side, taking her hand and drawing her back to sit beside him on the settee. Not releasing his grip on her fingers, he looked deep into her bewildered amber eyes, his voice huskily intent as he went on.

'What I actually said was that by leaving you stopped *me* making the biggest mistake of my life. But, remember, that was when I thought you'd left to be with Pete. What you didn't know is that the day before you went I had finally made up my mind to have all the medical tests I needed.'

'But why?'

'So that if I was in the clear—as I prayed I would be— I could ask you to marry me knowing that we could have children after all.'

'You... You wanted to marry me?'

'It was the thing I wanted most in the world, and it scared me.'

'Scared? You?'

It was hard to believe that Morgan, self-sufficient Morgan who had always seemed strong as a rock, should have been a prey to the same sort of uncertainties that had plagued her.

But he was nodding slowly, the sombre cast of his features leaving her in no doubt that this was the truth.

'I didn't know all that much about love. I'd hardly had the best sort of teachers, after all, and so I went about it all wrong. I should have talked to you about my past, about my father, but I didn't know how. To be honest, I thought you were better not knowing. That if it was just going to be a casual thing then there was no need for you to know. But then I realised that casual was something it could never be—not for me. You were the love of my life, and no one else would ever come close. And then I desperately wanted to protect you from the truth. At least until I knew it was the truth.'

Ruefully he shook his dark head in despair at the mistakes he had made.

'But I covered myself too well and as a result you didn't dare to tell me you were pregnant and I missed the first year of my daughter's life.'

'Morgan.' Ellie's voice was very soft. 'I wish I'd known.'

'And I wish I'd told you.'

He lifted her hands to his mouth, pressing a tender kiss on each of her fingers in turn, and Ellie felt her heart clench on a wave of love for him that was stronger than anything she had ever felt in her life before.

'I'm still scared,' he told her, the admission bringing tears to her eyes. 'But I'm going to try…'

'But…'

Ellie shook her head dazedly, not quite sure how much of what she was hearing she could believe.

'But you said to Rosie that she was your trump card, that…'

'You heard that? Then you only heard part of it, angel. Yes, I wanted to get to you through Rosie, but only as a beginning. If I could have nothing else, I wanted you there in my bed in the hope that one day, if I was truly lucky, it would come to mean more. That one day you might come to love me, as I loved you, and I was coming to love Rosie. What I wanted most in all the world was to be able to care for you—and this little girl I didn't know was my daughter.'

'That's what I want too,' Ellie said softly. 'We'll do it together.'

'Together?' Morgan sounded dazed and in his eyes hope warred with disbelief so that she had to rush to put him out of his misery.

'Morgan, you are the love of my life too. But when you

said you wanted me to marry you, I thought it was only because of Rosie—because you felt you had a duty to her.'

'No way!'

If she had had any room left for doubt, then the vehemence of his declaration would have convinced her.

'Ellie, I adore my daughter, I'd die to protect a single hair on her gorgeous little head, but one day she's going to grow up and lead her own life. The love I'd have for my wife is different. It's a lifetime thing, a one and only and for always. When I said I wanted to marry you, that was what I had in mind.'

'In that case, how could I possibly refuse?'

She was gathered into his arms, crushed against his chest, and his mouth took hers with all the passionate intensity that had been in his words. Instant heat rushed through her, making her senses swim, and she kissed him back with all the love that was in her heart.

At long last, Morgan lifted his head to draw in a much-needed breath.

'I'm the luckiest man in the world, with two gorgeous women in my life. I couldn't ask for anything more, except...'

His sudden stillness had Ellie lifting her head from the pillow of his chest to turn questioning bronze eyes on him.

'What is it?'

'Ellie, when exactly is Rosie's birthday?'

'At the end of the month—October twenty-fourth.'

'Perfect.' Morgan's tone was rich with contented satisfaction. 'How about making it a double celebration—Rosie's birthday and our wedding day?'

Her heart soared, and her smile was all the answer he needed.

'I can't think of anything that would make me happier. Though I have to admit that you've been very clever.'

'Clever?' Morgan frowned his confusion. 'How's that?'

'This way you'll always have a ready-made reminder of the date of our wedding anniversary in the future,' Ellie teased softly.

'I won't need a reminder,' Morgan assured her deeply, lowering his mouth to hers again. 'How could I ever forget the day that the best part of my life really began?'

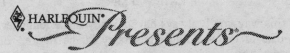

HARLEQUIN *Presents*

**The world's bestselling romance series.
Seduction and passion guaranteed!**

**Pick up a Harlequin Presents® novel and you will
enter a world of spine-tingling passion and
provocative, tantalizing romance!**

Join us in 2002 for an exciting selection of titles
from all your favorite authors:

HARLEQUIN®

*M*akes any time special ®

Visit us at www.eHarlequin.com

HPDECPRE

MISTRESS TO A MILLIONAIRE

She's his in the bedroom,
but he can't buy her love....

The ultimate fantasy becomes a reality
in

HARLEQUIN® *Presents*

Live the dream with more *Mistress to a Millionaire*
titles by your favorite authors.

Coming in March
THE BILLIONAIRE AFFAIR
by
Diana Hamilton #2238

Harlequin Presents®
The world's bestselling romance series.
Seduction and passion guaranteed!

Available wherever Harlequin books are sold.

HARLEQUIN®
Makes any time special®

If you enjoyed what you just read,
then we've got an offer you can't resist!

Take 2 bestselling
love stories FREE!
Plus get a FREE surprise gift!

Coming Next Month

THE BEST HAS JUST GOTTEN BETTER!

#2235 THE ITALIAN'S WIFE Lynne Graham

Rio Lombardi, managing director of Lombardi Industries, has an outburst of conscience. He insists that Holly, a homeless single mother, stay at his luxurious home. Rio then proceeds to lavish her and her baby with all that money can buy. But his emotions are caught off guard....

#2236 THE SECRET VENGEANCE Miranda Lee

While searching for his father's mistress, Luke Freeman has information that leads him to Celia. This beautiful young woman is not who he's looking for—but he has to have her all the same....

#2237 A WHIRLWIND MARRIAGE Helen Brooks

Marianne's marriage to Zeke Buchanan had been blissfully happy until recently—now somehow she had the feeling she was losing him.... Had they married too soon, too impulsively? Marianne was determined to fight to keep her husband's love!

#2238 THE BILLIONAIRE AFFAIR Diana Hamilton

Powerful businessman Ben Dexter had forgone a wife and family for years, ever since Caroline Harvey had betrayed him. But now it was time to get her out of his system. He would find her, indulge in an affair with her—and then get on with his life....

#2239 THE MISTRESS'S CHILD Sharon Kendrick

Lisi has never told Philip Caprice that their evening of passion resulted in a baby—until now. Philip's solution is that Lisi and their son move in with him—but is he only playing at happy families?

#2240 ROME'S REVENGE Sara Craven

Rome d'Angelo could have had his pick of women—only, his fiancée had already been chosen for him, by his grandfather. A family feud meant Rome was forced to make Cory Grant his bride and then jilt her. But his plans were spoiled when he discovered that he genuinely liked Cory....

HPCNM0202R